MOUNTWOOD SCHOOL FOR GHOSTS

TOBY IBBOTSON

from an original idea by

EVA IBBOTSON

MACMILLAN CHILDREN'S BOOKS

First published 2014 by Macmillan Children's Books

This edition published 2015 by Macmillan Children's Books
an imprint of Pan Macmillan
20 New Wharf Road, London N1 9RR
Associated companies throughout the world
www.panmacmillan.com

ISBN 978-1-4472-7101-7

MOUNTWOOD SCHOOL FOR GHOSTS

'Cue heaps of haunting mayhem and silliness. A triumph' *Daily Mail*

'Cleverly plotted and smoothly written' *Scotsman*

'This debut has confidence, panto characters to love and hate and a wonderfully peculiar sense of humour' *The Times*

For Ma

Contents

PART ONE   1

1   The Trouble with Ghosts   3

2   Great-Aunt Joyce   13

3   Lawless Lands   20

4   The Peabodys Make Plans   30

5   Percy   40

6   Mountwood   45

7   Charlotte's Quest   51

8   Journey by Moonlight   60

PART TWO   71

9   Jack Bluffit   73

10 Bad News   79

11 The Shortener   85

12 Saving Markham Street   92

13 Lord Ridget   99

14 The Dark of the Moon   107

15 Mrs Wilder Speaks Out   113

16 Pathetic Percy   123

17 Iffy Breaks the Rules   131

18 The Markham Street March   146

19 Bonding   155

PART THREE   159

20 In the Nick   161
21 Drainpipe and Rolling Pin   169
22 Lunatics   173
23 Noses and Thumbs   179
24 The Terrifying Worms   185
25 Heavy Machinery   194
26 Team Spectre   201
27 The Phantom Welder   206
28 Jinxed   215
29 Mr Jaros Waits   224
30 Number Six   233
31 After the Battle   247

PART ONE

One
The Trouble with Ghosts

Most people know what a hag is. They used to be common enough in every parish in the land. Any old lady who lived alone in a cave by the sea or a tumbledown cottage in marshland or forest might be a hag. If she had a wrinkly face, bushy eyebrows, a gobber tooth, a squint eye, a squawky voice, a scolding tongue and a cat, then she probably *was* a hag. And if she had hair growing on the inside of her mouth, then there was no doubt about it.

But there are also Great Hagges. They are spelled differently because they are quite rare. You won't find a Great Hagge living in a half-ruined bothy on a wuthering heath. You are more likely to find one living in a pleasant ground-floor flat in north Oxford. On the outside they are less fierce and disgusting than common hags; they are less hairy, and much bigger. But, inside, a Great Hagge is far more interesting and dangerous and full of ideas.

An ordinary village hag goes out at night to sit on people whom she doesn't like and stop them breathing, so that they wake in a panic. That's why some people look hag-ridden when they come down to breakfast. Great Hagges cannot be bothered with stuff like that. They dress properly (they like tweed), they make plans. They organize and put things right. They can't help it; that's the way they are. But putting

3

things right is not the same as being nice. Great Hagges aren't nice. They aren't do-gooders. Nothing like that. None of your knitting scarves for tramps or founding homes for stray kittens. They don't like people (not live ones, anyway; they enjoy a nibble of human flesh if it's properly cooked) – but they don't not like them either. It's just that for a Great Hagge it is quite impossible to ignore a mess, and most human beings are in a mess. People have feelings that get them into trouble. They feel sorry for other people who are ill or sad, they fall in love and out of love with each other, they worry about doing the right thing.

But of course the biggest and most stupid messes are made by politicians and heads of schools and people with more money than sense. Their messes mess up everybody else, and those are the kind that Great Hagges simply cannot abide.

So, if you meet a large fierce lady with a loud voice, who is bossier than the bossiest person you have ever met; a member of a parliamentary committee, or headmistress of a school for rich girls, or chairwoman of a hospital trust – she just *might* be a Great Hagge. But then again she might not be. After all, lots of important bossy ladies who are ordinary human beings have one long eyebrow and knobbly knees and huge feet. You would have to get up close to be sure. If you ever saw a Great Hagge in a swimsuit you would know instantly what she was. But that is not very likely to happen.

One Wednesday afternoon about a hundred years ago three Great Hagges met for tea; they were old friends, and they liked to stay in contact and exchange news.

4

Their real names were Fredegonda, Goneril and Drusilla, though those were not the names by which they were known. Fredegonda was chairwoman of the board of a high-security prison for serious offenders; she was tall and bony, with big front teeth, and had to have her shoes specially made because her feet were on the large side even for a Great Hagge. She also had a special thumb. It ran in the family, because she was descended on her mother's side from the great Irish hero Finn McCool. She had never been known to lose her temper, but when she told some wicked murderer in her icy voice that he should 'get a grip' or 'pull his socks up', then he almost always became as gentle as a lamb.

Goneril was principal of a college of nursing. She was not as tall as Fredegonda, but she was a lot wider and very strong and solid, and possessed a rather particular eye, the left one. Her nickname among the student nurses in her charge was the 'Wardrobe', but none of them ever used it within miles of her, because she *did* lose her temper sometimes, and the results were horrifying – things happened that were hard to explain.

The reason for this, of course, was that all Great Hagges can curse and spellbind if they wish to, and when they lose their temper, then they do sometimes wish to.

The third Great Hagge, Drusilla, was a Lifetime President of the Society for the Preservation of the British Heritage. She cared very deeply about the woods and rivers and hills and old houses of Britain. Drusilla had frizzy hair, a twinkly eye and a rosebud mouth, and her head was as round as the full moon.

5

But anybody who thought she was a softy was in for a nasty surprise. She was more practical and artistic than the other two, and she could be quite un-Haggeish sometimes. She had smoked a cigarette once, and on another occasion danced a tango at a New Year's Eve party with a gentleman from South America, a flower between her teeth. Luckily he was quite short, so her nose was well above his head and he was in no serious danger of being skewered in the eye. For her nose was no ordinary nose.

The three friends had worked very hard all their lives (Hagges have very long lives), sorting out various messes, and educating, and putting things right, and on this particular Wednesday, in the drawing room of Goneril's Bloomsbury flat, they made a momentous decision.

'My dears,' said Fredegonda, sipping her tea, 'I think the time has come. Enough is enough.'

The other two nodded. Great Hagges are tough, but even a Great Hagge gets tired eventually. It is absolutely exhausting telling other people what to do all day; any teacher will tell you that. So that afternoon the three friends decided that it was time to retire at last. They would return to nature and spend their last remaining years in peace, enjoying simple pleasures. Drusilla knew of a comfortable cave in the far north-west of Britain. She had spent her summer holidays there as a schoolgirl.

A few days later all three of them resigned from their important jobs and moved.

Their cave lay on the very shore of the great western ocean. At low tide, a crescent of silver-white sand stretched before the mouth of the cave. When the tide was high the beetling black cliffs of the headland plunged sheer into the surf, the cries of terns and skuas pierced the breakers' roar and seawater swirled soothingly around the ankles of the three companions as they sat enjoying their afternoon tea in the living room; Great Hagges do love to keep their feet damp. It was like living in paradise. They went for walks on the beach, gathering cockles and exploring rock pools. Drusilla found a sea slug and kept him as pet. She called him Mr Perkins, because he looked like the owner of a railway company with whom she had once had to be very firm; so firm, in fact, that he didn't survive the experience.

'We gave him such a moving send-off,' she said to her companions. 'I arranged the floral tributes myself.'

They got to know some of the locals. A couple of kelpies lived nearby, and the Mar-Tarbh, Dread Creature of the Sea, came over sometimes from Iona to say hello and exchange gossip.

For many years, ninety-seven to be precise, they lived their quiet life, while the world outside moved on. The three Great Hagges of the North became a rumour, a mere memory preserved among the ghosts, ghouls, sprites and other inhabitants of invisible Britain.

As far as the crofters and fishermen of the island were concerned, the Great Hagges kept themselves to themselves. But of course they met them sometimes, and said 'good morning' or 'nice weather today'. The people of the Western Isles are not the prying kind, and they are lot cannier about what goes on in the other world than most of us. They might have sat by their peat fires of an evening and wondered a bit about the large strange ladies who had taken up residence among them, but they knew better than to poke their noses into what didn't concern them.

The world might have forgotten them, but the Great Hagges had not forgotten the world. They kept themselves well-informed. They made good use of the library bus which came to the other side of their island once a month and they took a Sunday newspaper. They were not often pleased with what they read.

'It really is outrageous,' declared Fredegonda.

'Preposterous,' said Goneril.

'Pitiful,' said Drusilla.

Fredegonda had just finished reading aloud an article from the 'New Books for Young Readers' section of the newspaper. It started: 'This delightful tale of ghosts and spectres will charm readers of all ages . . .' and went on about a book in which the ghosts were funny and cute and friendly and a lot more besides.

'It is unendurable,' Fredegonda continued, 'to see the glorious traditions of ghosthood in this land trodden into the dust. Chummy spectres, plastic Halloween masks, gooey teenage vampires . . . there is no end to it. The vampires I have known certainly weren't gooey. Positively scary, I assure you.'

Drusilla and Goneril exchanged a little smile. The idea of Fredegonda being scared was very amusing. But they understood what she meant.

'The woman who wrote that book should be

flogged. "Delightful" indeed! Centuries of hard haunting being spat upon.'

'Ridiculed,' said Drusilla.

'Mocked and derided,' agreed Goneril. 'On the other hand,' she went on, 'I do think that the ghosts of Britain are partly to blame. They have become enfeebled and sloppy. I haven't heard of a single person who has been frightened to death by ghosts in the last ten years. Frightened – yes. But to death – no.'

'True enough,' said Fredegonda. 'Standards have fallen everywhere. The ghosts of Great Britain have been dragged down along with everything else – they no longer understand the meaning of hard work. A professional haunting requires more than just vaguely floating about. Those ghosts must get a grip.'

All three Hagges shook their heads and tutted.

'Time for a cup of tea,' said Drusilla, and she got up to make a brew.

Tea always helps one to think, especially when accompanied by a nice plate of sponge fingers. Drusilla's fingers were particularly tasty. She prepared them herself from a recipe she had got from her mother, and they were a special treat, because it was not easy to get hold of fingers nowadays. Drowned fishermen were becoming scarce, what with all the newfangled navigation aids and coastal rescue helicopters.

'Delicious as usual, Drusilla,' said Fredegonda. 'Now, I have been thinking, ladies, and we must act. We may be retired, we may not be as young as we used to be –' this was undoubtedly true, Fredegonda having just celebrated her four-hundred-and-seventy-third birthday, which is oldish even for a Great Hagge – 'but our work is not done. Unseen Britain is in a mess. We have a duty.'

The other two looked at her expectantly. To them, words like 'duty' and 'work' were like 'walkies' or 'fetch' to a dog. If they had had tails, they would have wagged them. But Great Hagges don't have tails.

'We must establish a training school for the ghosts of Great Britain,' Fredegonda went on. 'They must be re-educated. They must relearn the ancient skills. Haunting, terrifying, cursing ... proper cursing of course, not just rude words.'

'Of course! Education is the answer!' cried Goneril, as she had cried many a time when addressing her trainee nurses.

'A vital part of our heritage must be preserved!' boomed Drusilla, glaring fiercely from under her eyebrow, as she had so often done when confronting developers and do-gooders.

And so the Great Hagges made their plans.

There is a tremendous amount to do if you want to start a training school, or rather an Institute of Higher Education, which is how the Great Hagges described their project. There has to be a syllabus with courses in different subjects, a timetable, a proper system for marking and assessment, and lots of rules and regulations. But first and foremost there has to be an actual school building. So the first thing the Great Hagges had to do was find the right place. And because they were the kind of persons who got things done, and didn't just talk about them, they set out the very next day.

The weather was glorious. The sea sparkled and danced, lapping the white sands and heaving gently against the rocks. An old bull seal lazed out in the bay, his great sleek head bobbing in the swell. The Hagges were quite sad to leave, but at the same time they were very excited about what lay ahead. They enjoyed their quiet life, but they were Improvers at heart, and they hadn't bossed anybody around for almost a hundred years. So they were in high spirits as they turned inland and marched in single file across the peaty bogs and springy heather to the other side of the island, where they could catch the boat to the mainland.

On the outskirts of the little harbour town was an old stone barn, and when they reached it Goneril produced a large rusty key and opened the doors. Inside was a car. It was a bit dusty, but the midnight-blue paintwork still glowed with the deep hue that is the mark of countless hours of polishing by skilled human hands. On the front of the long bonnet was a small silver figurine: a goddess, or a spirit, with outstretched wings.

'Will it start?' asked Fredegonda.

'I jolly well hope so,' said Goneril, 'The man who sold it to me said that it was a high-quality vehicle.'

It was in fact a 1912 Rolls-Royce Silver Ghost, which Goneril had purchased mainly because she liked the name. They dusted off the cream leather seats and climbed in, with Goneril behind the wheel. The engine came instantly to life, settling into a quiet purr like a contented puma. The man who had sold it was obviously speaking the truth about its quality, for it had stood unused since 1923, when the Hagges had taken it to visit Drusilla's aunt, then in her six hundred and nineteenth year and poorly. She had had an interesting life. In 1388, as a young Hagge, she had been present at the battle of Otterburn, helping the Scots fight the English army by casting spells and howling imprecations. She had enjoyed herself tremendously. It was probably thanks to her efforts that the Scots had won in spite of being heavily outnumbered.

The ferry was on time and the crossing was calm. As the Rolls headed south towards the English border Drusilla, who was in the back seat, produced a bag of bullseyes for them to suck on.

'Do you know,' she said, 'I saw that they were selling bulls' eyes in that little sweetshop on the quayside.'

'But they are only peppermints, dear. You know, sweets. Not proper ones like yours, and not nearly as nice.'

'Oh, silly me,' Drusilla giggled. Her giggle was rather an odd sound, halfway between the screaming bark of a dog fox and the scraping of fingernails on a blackboard. It had surprised quite a lot of people in the days when she had been invited to dinner parties in London. But the other two were used to it, and in a cheerful mood of adventure the hunt began.

Two
Great-Aunt Joyce

Daniel Salter lived in Markham Street, at number six. It was his home, and most of the time he didn't think about it; he just lived there. But now, sitting on the top step outside his front door as the evening shadows lengthened, he thought about it. He thought about what it would be like to live somewhere else. Markham Street lay in a big industrial town in the far north of England, and there were lots of streets that Daniel definitely did not want to live in. Streets with small houses on big thoroughfares where the rush-hour traffic crawled morning and evening, and roared past the rest of the day, filling the air with exhaust fumes. In a street like that nobody could have a cat; it would be run over in no time. And there were often no gardens, or only tiny bits of garden at the front, and they were usually concreted over so that people could park their cars. And there was nowhere for birds to live.

But in Markham Street he could sit quietly and watch the big tabby from next door trying to sneak up on an unsuspecting blackbird that was poking about in the flower bed, quite unaware that death was stalking up on it. If he clapped his hands he would startle the bird and save its life, but that would be disturbing the course of nature.

This isn't the course of nature, though; it's just

unfair, thought Daniel. It wasn't as though the tabby was a wild animal trying to survive. It was spoiled and overfed and its name was Tompkins, and any minute now Mrs Cranford would come out and call it in for supper.

At that moment Daniel's mother opened the door behind him and said, 'It's time to come in now, Daniel.'

The blackbird flew off in a flurry of dark wings, and Tompkins looked miffed and stalked off.

Daniel sighed deeply and got up to go inside. The best thing about Markham Street was that you could be outside a lot. The houses were all on one side of the street. Opposite them was a strip of grass, and then a wooden fence. Beyond the fence were the grounds of a large building that had once been a brewery and now housed some offices. On the property were tall sycamore and horse chestnut trees. The children of Markham Street weren't really allowed to be there, but after office hours they often were, kicking balls against the doors of the garages, or looking for conkers. The younger children chalked hopscotch squares right in the middle of the street, and the older ones played football, and when a car did come it drove very slowly and there was plenty of time to get out of the way. Markham Street was a cul-de-sac. At the top of the street was a row of black-painted iron posts, at least a hundred years old, with space between them for people and dogs and bicycles and pushchairs, but not cars. Daniel spent as much time as he possibly could out in the street, or over at some neighbour's house, usually his best friend Charlotte's. He liked his own house, and he absolutely loved his mother and his father. But his house contained Great-Aunt Joyce.

There are a lot of great-aunts in the world who are very nice, sending interesting presents at Christmas, and telling stories about what it was like to travel on steam trains and ocean liners and have porters to carry your luggage. Great-Aunt Joyce was not one of those. She was nasty, thoroughly one-hundred-per-cent horrid. Daniel was grown-up enough to know that nobody is perfect. Some people are a bit greedy, or a bit snobbish, or a bit grumpy. Great-Aunt Joyce was totally greedy and snobbish and grumpy and mean and a lot of other things.

She had come to live with them years ago, when Daniel was very small, because she was in some kind of trouble and had nowhere else to go. Now she was just there, like an incurable disease. She told Daniel off all the time, she complained about everything, she left her used knickers outside her bedroom door for Daniel's mother to wash and she suffered from varicose veins. That wasn't her fault. But when she sat in the best chair in the front room she rolled down her stockings, put her feet up on the coffee table and massaged her legs, which *was* her fault. She made life miserable for Daniel. The most miserable thing was that she was allergic to everything. Not only to dust and pollen, but to everything; this meant that Daniel could never have a pet. Not a dog, not a cat, not a hamster, not a budgerigar. Anything with hair or feathers made her face swell up and her eyes water and brought her out in a rash. That's what she said, anyway, but Daniel suspected she was just making it up; his mother remembered visiting her as a child, and then she had a cat that used to sit on the sofa and shed hair all over the place.

'I suppose all her troubles brought it on. That can happen, you know,' said Mrs Salter.

Daniel had a friend called Mike who lived at number eleven. Mike was often in trouble because he was interested in things. If he saw something interesting on the other side of someone's fence, he would climb over to take a look, and if it was *very* interesting he would take it home to look at more closely. Daniel hated to be in trouble, but for Mike it was just something that happened, like rain or grazing your knee. People on the street muttered that his father treated him badly, but he just shrugged his shoulders. Daniel felt a bit sorry for him sometimes, but more often he was jealous. Mike had an aquarium in his bedroom and two or three cages with small animals in them. He had even had a pet jackdaw for a while, which he had found as a fledgling and fed on worms and mince.

'But Great-Aunt Joyce can't be allergic to grass snakes,' Daniel said to his mother one day, after another visit to the pet shop with Mike, who was getting food for his gerbil. 'Or goldfish. They have aquariums in doctors' waiting rooms.'

'Oh, Daniel, you know she has a phobia about snakes. And goldfish food does things to her lungs,' said his mother. 'Please don't make a fuss.'

Daniel tried not to make a fuss, because he knew that his mother suffered almost as much from Great-Aunt Joyce as he did. But he spent a lot of time out of the house, and so did his father, who had an allotment by the railway line at the bottom of the hill where the

16

vegetables were very well looked after indeed, and there was a little shed that had lots of stuff in it that weren't anything to do with gardening, like books and CDs.

Markham Street was a street of terraced houses, big old houses which had once been homes for quite rich people, so there were lots of rooms on top of each other, and lots of stairs. At the top of the houses were attic rooms that had once been for the servants, and lower down were the big rooms for the doctors and lawyers and businessmen who had owned the houses, and the kitchens were right at the bottom at the back, because making the food wasn't something well-off people did so people used to have cooks. Food just arrived on the table.

But now things were different, and the big old kitchen was the place where Daniel's family cooked, and ate, and talked.

'Broccoli,' said Great-Aunt Joyce, as Daniel's mother brought the food to the table. 'You know I have difficulty with cabbage. Broccoli is no better.'

'But it's fresh from the allotment, Aunt Joyce. John brought it in this afternoon.'

'I'm afraid that makes no difference. I shall probably suffer pangs tonight. You could fill a hot-water bottle for me this evening, and bring me some hot milk. That might ease the pain.'

Daniel ate in silence, as fast as he could.

'Don't wolf down your food, Daniel,' said Great-Aunt Joyce. 'You are quite spoiling the little appetite I have left.'

Joyce's appetite was not entirely spoiled. There was rice pudding for afters, and first she said that she could possibly try just a tiny bit, and then she felt she could manage just a tiny bit more. In the end she had three full helpings, and Daniel, who loved rice pudding, hardly got any.

'Can I leave the table now?' asked Daniel.

'Well you *can*,' said Great-Aunt Joyce. 'The question is whether you *may*.' She prided herself on being a bit of a stickler for correct grammar.

'Off you go, Daniel,' said his father.

Daniel went up to his room and shut the door. He had an attic room right at the top of the house, with a window that looked out over the street. It was the only place in the whole house which was not a Great-Aunt Joyce danger zone.

Daniel sat on the low windowsill and looked out over the roof slates to the street below. It was getting dark, and soon the street lamps would be lit. To his right he could see down into Mrs Cranford's well-kept garden, where the delphiniums glowed bright blue in the evening light. On the other side the garden was overgrown, and what had once been a well-tended patch of lawn was full of dandelions and daisies.

This house had stood empty for several months, with a 'For Sale' sign on a post by the hedge. He and Charlotte had talked quite a lot about what kind of people would move in. Daniel was hoping for an old couple who needed someone to walk their dog, or at least a family with some children of his age. Charlotte wanted someone a bit different, from a foreign country.

'They might be Romany who are fleeing oppression in Eastern Europe,' Charlotte had said hopefully. She had been reading about them. 'And their children will dance and play the violin and be good with horses.'

'Where will they keep a horse?' said Daniel. 'In the living room, I suppose.'

Charlotte had frowned. Sometimes Daniel could be a bit of a sourpuss. But she knew all about Great-Aunt Joyce of course, and she realized that his life was not an easy one.

Daniel went to bed that night feeling sorry for himself. It seemed that the really interesting and exciting things that happened to other people were never going to happen to him. He was wrong.

Three
Lawless Lands

The Great Hagges were having tea.

'Well,' said Fredegonda, 'this is turning out to be rather a bother.'

'It certainly is,' Goneril agreed. 'We can hardly offer an advanced course in howling and moaning next door to a cinema showing a film called *Screams of the Damned*.

They had just visited an empty warehouse on the outskirts of a large city. But the smarmy estate agent who had taken them there hadn't mentioned the huge multiplex cinema nearby. They had spent many days touring the length and breadth of the country, trying to find a suitable place for their school of ghosthood, but it was proving difficult.

Britain had changed quite a lot since they last went motoring. The Ordnance Survey map that was in the glove compartment of the Rolls was very little use. Towns and cities had got much bigger, there were huge roads where there should be open countryside, and there were even completely new towns, such as Milton Keynes and Welwyn Garden City, which weren't marked on their map at all. And although there were plenty of places for sale or rent, most of them were far too modern and filled with things that ghosts, ghouls and spectres really have no use for at all, such as en-suite bathrooms with flushing

toilets and central heating. Even wh
decided only to look at old castles, disus
and abandoned hotels, the buildings were
close to a town or a golf course or a railway

Luckily Great Hagges don't need a lot o.
and none at all when they have important w. to
do. But they do need tea. So now they were sitting
in a small cafe in a pleasant tree-lined street. They
had had some very unpleasant experiences looking
for a decent place to stop, and they shuddered when
they thought of the way they had seen young people
behave, and adults too for that matter. Once they had
even been served by a girl with a ring in her nose
like a prize porker and another one in her lip and yet
another in her eyebrow. Times had certainly changed,
and not entirely for the better. But the little tea shop
which they had found now was bearable, just a few
tables with proper tablecloths and doilies on the
saucers and some older customers chatting quietly to
each other. They had ordered a pot of tea for three
and a plate of scones, and been served by a pleasant
middle-aged woman who didn't have metal in her
face.

'Perhaps we should just accept that it's hopeless,'
said Drusilla. Of the three of them, she was the one
who most missed the comforts of home, especially
her kitchen.

'Don't be a weed, Drusilla. We must soldier on.'

But even Fredegonda, who was the eldest and
most determined, was beginning to have her doubts.

It was late afternoon when they left the cafe, and as
they drove, darkness fell. They pressed on through

21

night, Goneril driving and Fredegonda reading the map. Drusilla was dozing in the back.

Goneril was a good driver, and the Rolls had a fine turn of speed. Suddenly in the headlights they saw a car with flashing blue lights on the roof parked at the side of the road. Beside it a figure in uniform was holding up his hand.

'I think there's been an accident. We'd better see what's going on.' Goneril braked and stopped.

The uniformed figure walked over to the Rolls.

'Are you in trouble, officer?' asked Goneril, sticking her head out of the driver's window.

'It's you who are in trouble,' came the reply. 'You were doing seventy-five.'

'I don't think that's anything to worry about. In fact she's going nicely, considering her age.'

'Very funny. Show me your licence, please.'

'My licence? What are you talking about? You are being rather impertinent, young man.'

Goneril had bought her car long before people had to take driving tests.

'Either you produce a licence, or I shall arrest you for illegal driving. Step out of the car.'

Policemen have very thorough training before they are let out to start policing. They are taught how to deal with violent drunks, armed bank robbers and belligerent teenagers. But nothing in their training tells them what to do when confronted with three Great Hagges in a speeding Rolls-Royce.

If he had been properly trained, this particular policeman would probably not have tried to arrest Goneril, and he would definitely never, ever have *told* her to get out of the car. He would have asked her politely, and added that vital word 'please'. A Great Hagge can be both generous and forgiving, but simply will not be told.

'I beg your pardon?' said Goneril, and a small child would have heard something in her voice that promised no good to come. But policemen are not small children, they are grown-up men in uniforms, and hearing that sort of thing is not their strong point.

'You heard me. Get out,' said the policeman.

So what followed was simply unavoidable. It started down at his feet. Suddenly his shoes seemed very tight. And then he felt that his trousers were several sizes too small, and his shirt. His collar started to strangle him, and he went very red in the face and began to splutter and gasp for air. By now his whole head, which had been on the small side, was the size of a football, then a party balloon. He was swelling up, just as though somebody had attached him to an air hose. Then the splitting started, which was lucky for him, or he would have choked to death. Sounds of ripping and tearing could be heard, and as he got bigger and bigger his uniform fell off him in shreds. In less than a minute a huge round pale naked policeman was standing in the road, looking very much like a hot-air balloon about to fly away. His police hat, strangely, remained balanced like a little blue fly right on top of his vast head.

It was Drusilla's voice from the back of the car that saved his life.

'Oh, Goneril, please don't burst him, dear; there will be such a terrible mess.'

With an effort Goneril calmed herself, and the

23

white of her left eye, which always turned green when she was spellbinding, returned to normal. She snorted, put the car into gear and drove off.

Fredegonda had been silent all this time, but now she spoke. 'Well, that settles it. We'll have to go home now. We can't stay here. Really, Goneril, a bit more self-control is to be expected from someone of your experience.'

'You're making too much of it,' said Goneril. 'He will start deflating in an hour or two.'

'It won't make much difference what size he is. You cannot leave a naked policeman in the middle of the road without questions being asked. They will be out looking for us in no time, and the car is not exactly inconspicuous.'

Goneril said nothing. Her eyes were fixed firmly on the road ahead. She was still upset. But she was also a bit ashamed of herself. She had always respected the authorities, and if they had been stopped by a policewoman, and not a policeman, then things might have turned out very differently. One of the very few things that had pleased the Hagges about the modern world was the advancement of women. The first time they saw a lady police officer they had been very excited.

'That I should live to see the day!' Drusilla had exclaimed. At one time she had fought hard for the rights of women.

But now there was nothing for it. They left the main road at the next turning and started to make their way by the shortest possible route back to the Scottish border. In the pale light of dawn they saw drystone walls marching over sweeping moorland pastures, and heard the cry of the curlew. Stone byres and cottages huddled in the valleys out of the wind. They were in the borderlands.

They came to yet another fork in the narrow winding road.

'Left or right?' asked Goneril, bringing the car to a halt.

Fredegonda, sitting with the map on her knees in the front passenger seat, was silent. She was lost. She hated to admit it. She had always prided herself on her map-reading skills, but the ancient map and the maze of country lanes had defeated her. To make things worse, the morning mist still lay on the hills and it was impossible to get her bearings.

Drusilla sat up in the back seat and sniffed. 'Let's go left. I like the smell of it.'

Soon they were driving through the Debatable Lands, a part of the country that for hundreds of years was neither England or Scotland, but a lawless tract where outlaws and bandits and fierce clan leaders held sway, stealing sheep, feuding and pillaging, both to the north and to the south, and then retreating by secret pathways over the moors to their fortified peel towers.

Drusilla had taken over the navigation, and now they followed her nose, which she stuck out of the window. Something in the air was drawing her on, something that whispered to her of damp leaf mould, rotting flesh, mouse droppings, decomposition and decay. It was irresistible to Drusilla, reminding her of happy afternoons in the kitchen trying out new recipes.

Suddenly she cried, 'Here, turn right here!' and

Goneril swung the car into a narrow lane that dived steeply downhill through a dense stand of fir trees.

They were descending into a narrow valley. On both sides dark crags were outlined against the sky, cutting out the light. The further in they drove, the gloomier it became. Just as Goneril was beginning to think that the track was turning into a path, and was starting to worry about her shock-absorbers, the valley opened out slightly, and before them, crouched darkly under an overhanging face of blackened rock, was a castle.

It wasn't a big castle, more a large rambling house, but it had battlements and slit windows. The ancient sandstone walls, gnawed by wind and rain, were adorned with waterlogged moss and slimy lichens.

The Great Hagges got out of the car and stood for a moment drawing the damp and foetid air deep into their lungs.

'Oh, how delightful,' said Fredegonda. 'Just imagine if . . .' She didn't have to finish her sentence. They were all thinking the same thing, and as one they approached the castle.

The ground around the building was squelchy – any drainpipes and gutters that had ever existed were long gone – and all three Hagges just longed to remove their sensible shoes and woollen stockings and feel ooze between their toes. But they didn't. Business must come before pleasure.

The front entrance had a big door of solid, iron-studded oak. It had been made to resist the attacks of bloodthirsty marauders from both sides of the border and was still in good shape. Beside it hung a bell pull on an iron chain. Goneril gave it a tug, and it came off in her hand.

'Oh dear,' she said.

'The place looks deserted,' said Drusilla. 'Shall we just have a peep inside?'

Goneril put the flat of her hand against the door and gave a little push. With a wrenching sound the two iron bars on the inside bent like rubber and sprang loose, and the door creaked inwards on its hinges.

Drusilla giggled. 'It seems to be open.'

The lower floor was a single stone-flagged vault, where livestock and women had been herded together for protection in troubled times. Cobwebs curtained the tiny windows set high in the walls, and a large rat scuttled along by the wall.

'This is very promising,' said Fredegonda, 'but we must not get our hopes up yet.'

On the floor was a big flat block of sandstone, with a ringbolt set into it. A chain had once been attached to the ringbolt, and two strong men, with the help of a wheel and ratchet, could lift the stone and expose the mouth of a well, which was the only source of water during a siege. Now Goneril walked forward and pushed the stone aside with the outside of her foot. She leaned over the dark well-mouth.

'Cooee, is there anyone at home?'

At first there was no answer. The only sound was a slow drip, drip, dripping. Then a pale bluish mist began to gather slowly on the black surface of the water at the bottom of the well. It swirled gently for a while, and finally became a face, hollowed-eyed, with

27

straggly hair and a half-open gap-toothed mouth.

It was the ghost of Angus Crawe, who had a great many dark deeds on his conscience, or would have had if he had a conscience. One evening he had got into a fight with his nephew over a young woman whom they had captured in a raid on Alnwick. He managed to slaughter his nephew, but slipped on the blood that splattered the floor and fell headlong into the well. His nephew's mates had quite simply put the cover-stone back and gone out to a party.

'Oh, there you are,' said Goneril. 'We are looking for the laird. Can you help us?'

The pale mouth moved, trying to form words, but Angus Crawe had not spoken for centuries, and his broad Northumbrian accent had not been easy to understand even when he was alive.

'Could you speak up, please? And try to articulate.'

'Eee . . . Eees . . . Eeble.' said Angus.

'What on earth are you saying, man?' Goneril was getting irritated. 'Eels? Eagles? Evil?'

Finally Angus produced a proper word. 'Peebles,' he said.

Goneril was very determined, and after a long question-and-answer session they worked out what they needed to know. The last laird of the castle came from a long line of uncouth border reivers and was no better than his wild ancestors. He had married a girl from the local town, who had soon discovered what a terrible mistake she had made, and being a resourceful lass she had doctored the brakes of his Land Rover. The very next day he tried to slow down as usual to take a bend at the bottom of a steep hill, but the Land

Rover just flew straight on and landed in the riverbed far below. The vehicle was totally demolished, and so was the laird. His wife inherited all his wealth, which was considerable, and left the hated home of her husband to rot. She was now enjoying a very expensive holiday at the Peebles Hydro, a holiday that had already lasted for several years.

The Hagges had found what they were looking for. Within a few days they had contacted the Peebles Hydro and been told in no uncertain terms that they were welcome to the dratted place and much good may it do them. The price was very reasonable. At first there were some delays caused by lawyers in Edinburgh who didn't seem to understand that there was no time to waste. But the Hagges paid them a visit, and after that everything went very quickly indeed. They moved in and were soon hard at work planning a curriculum and drafting important documents. The name of the castle was Mountwood, and within a surprisingly short period of time they were ready to open the doors and welcome the first students.

Four
The Peabodys Make Plans

'I feel,' said Ronald Peabody, 'That this is what we have been waiting for.'

He had been a tall well-muscled gentleman before he became a ghost, with a large handlebar moustache and side whiskers. Neither the moustache nor the whiskers were still there. They had been burned off in the fire that had turned him and his family into ghosts. Most of his skin had been burned off too, so that all his muscles could be clearly seen. He didn't mind that, because he was very proud of his muscles, biceps, triceps and all the rest, which he had worked very hard to develop. But he still pined dreadfully for his facial hair.

'We need to be constantly improving ourselves,' he went on. 'This is just the thing.'

Ronald and his wife Iphigenia were reading a notice that had suddenly appeared in glowing fiery letters on the wall of the travel agency where they lived, in between a big poster advertising Sun and Fun in Crete, and Weekend Breaks in Bratislava. A theatre had once stood on the site.

'No doubt you are right, dearest,' said Iphigenia.

'I am right, Iffy dear, I am,' said Ronald. 'We shall have a break from town life, breathe the country air and return renewed.'

Iphigenia had been an actress, a beautiful tragic

actress, and she had masses of wonderful copper-coloured hair. She had been lucky enough to die of smoke asphyxiation when the theatre went up in flames, rather than burning, and for this she thanked her lucky stars every day. If she had lost her hair, then death would not have been worth living.

The notice they had been reading said:

PUT THE GHASTLY BACK INTO GHOSTHOOD
RETURN THE HORROR TO HAUNTING
*The Mountwood Institute of Spectral Education offers
a refresher course in essential skills to all interested
members of the other side.*

Then came quite a lot of information about the different courses. 'Plashing and Moaning', 'The Wail for the Modern Era', 'Gnashing and Rattling', 'Basic Bloodcurdling', 'Exercising the Ectoplasm' and a seminar entitled 'Removal of body parts – the when and the where'.

Their son Perceval said nothing. He wasn't a very good reader yet, and he didn't quite get what they were talking about. He had passed on with his parents, which was a good thing, because he would have hated to be left an orphan. His mother had been performing a very tragic role on the night the theatre went up in flames, and he had been given a small part in the play. Dressed in a nightshirt he was lying in a crib being her starving son. He even had a line, 'Oh, mother dear, I die, I die.'

He could still remember it. When he said it the heroine was supposed to go out into the snow to beg for help, and lots of awful things would happen. But they never did, because just before he spoke smoke started seeping up through the boards of the stage, and someone shouted, 'Fire!'

'Just what we need, eh? Percy and I can do lots of sports, and work on our fitness, can't we, lad? We can go through the pain barrier.'

'Yes, Father.'

Ronald Peabody had once been a long-distance swimmer. He still wore the charred remnants of an old-fashioned woollen swimsuit that had been scorched into his body during the fatal fire. He did his best to encourage his son to care for his body. He gave Percy pep talks about the Fight for Fitness, and the War on Weakness, and Building your Body. He wasn't a stupid man, and he was well aware that Percy did not in fact have a body – none of them did – but it was the spirit of the thing that mattered, the manliness. And you don't need a body in order to have willpower.

It was Ronald who had started the fire in the theatre. Long-distance swimmers have to cover their whole bodies in grease to keep out the cold, and Ron had just returned from a swim up the Thames from Tower Bridge to Putney, still in his swimsuit, and was preparing to change in Iphigenia's dressing room and escort her home after the performance. But he came too close to a gaslight, and because he was covered in tallow he instantly ignited and blazed like a bonfire. It was a shame, but accidents happen. As Ron used to say, there is no point in crying over spilt milk. You just pick yourself, dust yourself off and start all over again.

There was something else though, something that

weighed on him even now after more than a hundred years, and made him absolutely determined that his son would have a Will of Steel. For Ronald Peabody had given way to weakness once, and it had led to a terrible disappointment. Even now he couldn't talk about it.

Percy wanted to please his father, and he always did his best. He wanted to please his mother too. But it wasn't easy to please both of them. His mother was artistic. She felt poetry very strongly, and Percy tried to feel it too, although he didn't always understand it.

'There is soul in you, Perceval, I know it, but it must be nurtured,' she would say.

Now Iphigenia read a bit more of the notice. 'Oh!' she exclaimed. 'Mountwood is in the north, near the Scottish border. What balm to the spirit to wander among the dales and hills, to see the daffodils nodding in the breeze. To feel nature's elemental power. Earth hath not anything to show more fair.'

'Eh? Sorry, dear, I wasn't attending,' said Ronald. 'I see they're providing transport. Mighty efficient, those Great Hagges. Motorway service station, stroke of midnight, day after tomorrow. We'd better be there.'

'Do you know,' said Iphigenia, 'I think I shall try to persuade Cousin Vera to join us. She has been looking frightfully pale and wan, and her vocal chords are simply wasting away.' Cousin Vera was a banshee, and for a banshee voice is everything.

Iphigenia vanished through the wall to have a word with Cousin Vera in the nearby graveyard where she lived.

*

One day when Daniel came home from school the 'For Sale' sign had gone from the next-door garden.

A few days later an enormous lorry with 'Forrest and Hills Ltd., Removals' on the side edged carefully into the street and stopped outside the empty house. A couple of burly men jumped out of the cab, lowered the tailgate and started shifting furniture out of the back, up the short path and into the house.

Daniel watched from his window. You can learn a lot about people from their furniture, and he wished that Charlotte was there so that they could talk about it, but when he rang her there was no answer.

The furniture which the grunting removal men were lugging up the front steps of number seven did not look very promising. Quite a lot of it – an oval dining table and a set of chairs, for example – was swathed in sheets of plastic and lots of tape, which meant that it was expensive and polished. There was a huge Welsh dresser that the men almost dropped on the path, and a sideboard, both made of very dark wood with thick legs. There was a standard lamp with a chintzy lampshade. There were lots of packing cases, and Daniel could only guess what they contained. There was a glass-fronted bookcase, the kind that has books in it that nobody ever reads, if it has books at all. It might just as easily contain a collection of glass bunny rabbits, or golfing trophies. Then came two matching beds with padded headboards.

No bicycles, no skateboards, no birdcages, no playpen, no dog bed and no violins. No horse.

No children, no animals and no Romany refugees for Charlotte. I might have known it, thought Daniel.

One last object was being dragged out of the back

of the lorry. It was an ugly chest of drawers with a curved front and brass handles. It was obviously meant to look like an expensive antique, and it obviously wasn't. But as Daniel watched the men heaving the heavy piece up the front steps, something odd occurred, something that he could never really explain, even to himself.

The chest of drawers that he was looking at went wavery and blurry. Then the wavery blur gathered itself into a sort of misty cloud, and the misty cloud swooshed in through the front door and disappeared.

Daniel rubbed his eyes. The whole thing had taken just a few seconds. But Daniel knew he had seen something very unusual. When people see something very unusual they know it. Afterwards, when they think about it, they often dismiss it. 'I was dizzy, I didn't have enough breakfast, I'm coming down with something, I was imagining things, I had strained my eyes,' they tell themselves. They forget that when they actually saw it, they knew. Daniel sat down on his bed, and his heart thumped. He knew.

At supper that evening Great-Aunt Joyce talked about their new neighbours. She occupied the biggest room in the house, naturally, with three big windows looking out over the street, and while Daniel had stood in his room looking at the furniture being unloaded next door, she had done the same thing on the floor below, sitting in her special comfy chair and peering out of the window. She spent much of the day there, disapproving of everything and hoping that a dog would lift its leg against the fence, or a child kick a ball into the garden, so that she could tell Daniel's father to complain.

'Well, I think they seem to be the right sort of people,' said Great-Aunt Joyce. 'They can't be foreigners, if their furniture is anything to go by. I must say that's a relief. I shall look in at some point and welcome them to our street. If I'm up to it, that is. If not, you must invite them over for coffee, Sarah. It is the proper thing to do.'

'Of course we will want to get to know them, Aunt Joyce,' said Daniel's mother. She hadn't seen the furniture, but she had heard about the new neighbours from Mrs Hughes at number nine, and she wasn't very hopeful. A dog to cheer Daniel up would have been better.

'Great-Aunt Joyce,' said Daniel, 'did you see anything a bit funny about the chest of drawers that they took in at the end?'

'Funny?' Aunt Joyce's fork, which had just speared a large piece of sausage, stopped on its way to her mouth. She leaned forward and pointed it at Daniel. 'What do you mean, boy?' Her eyes narrowed.

Although Daniel couldn't stand Aunt Joyce, he wasn't scared of her. But now, for a brief second, he was afraid. 'Nothing, I didn't mean anything. I just thought that it was a . . . a funny-looking piece of furniture.'

The moment passed. Aunt Joyce went on eating. 'It was a very nice piece,' she said. 'And no doubt very valuable. Chippendale, I think. Not that I would dream of prying into other people's personal property.'

Daniel said nothing. If Great-Aunt Joyce had seen

something too, then she wasn't going to tell him about it.

After breakfast the next day, Daniel went to talk to Charlotte. He knew where she would be, because it was Sunday, and every Sunday Charlotte took her small brothers to the park so that her mother could have a lie-in.

The park was another good thing about Markham Street. If you went through the posts at the top of the street and walked up a cobbled lane full of wheelie bins, past the back entrances of another row of houses, you came to the park. It was very big, with wide-open green spaces and lovely old trees and council flower beds where the park keepers planted pansies in special shapes, so that they formed pictures of the city's coat of arms, or the emblem of the football team.

The park was on the top of a hill, and there were views right across the city to the great cranes and gantries that still lined the river, even though nobody had built ships or loaded coal and steel there for years and years. You could see the spires of churches, and the high-rises on the other side of town. There was a shallow pond – an artificial lake, really. The water wasn't very clean, but some ducks lived there, and they seemed to get on all right. There were dense clumps of rhododendron. You could see a squirrel sometimes, but you were more likely to see a rat, and quite a lot of litter. It was the kind of park that visitors might think was a fairly grotty place. But for the children of Markham Street it was a playground, and breathing space, and freedom. For the parents of the children it was a blessing.

Right in the middle of the park, at the highest point, was a statue. It was a statue of General Sir George Markham, who had gone to the local grammar school and risen to fame in the army, finally being gloriously hacked to pieces at a famous last stand somewhere in Africa.

Charlotte Hamilton was sitting on the stone pedestal at the foot of the statue. She was a thinnish girl, just the right side of skinny, and she was a bit taller than Daniel, with long thick hair the colour of wheat. ('Old straw is more like it,' she used to say.)

She was reading, or trying to read. The wind kept blowing her hair into her face and ruffling the book's pages in an annoying way, and her youngest brother kept wandering off in the direction of the lake. The water was very shallow, but she still had to keep an eye on him. So she was quite happy to close her book and talk to Daniel instead when he flopped down beside her.

They talked about Daniel's new neighbours.

'Well, they might be interesting even though they have no children,' said Charlotte. 'And people with lots of children aren't exactly perfect neighbours. If it was us moving in, and they started unloading cots and high chairs and baby baths and tricycles, then I bet some people would be pretty upset. Where's Alexander?'

They found him under a rhododendron bush and walked down to the lake to get the worst of the dirt off him.

'They might be doctors who work in disaster areas and operate on people in tents, or helicopter pilots, or musicians or actors or mountaineers,' Charlotte went on.

'I bet you anything they aren't. Not with a leather armchair and a dining-table that two grown men can hardly lift. Great-Aunt Joyce says they are the "right sort of people".'

'Oh.'

There was nothing to say to that.

They collected Charlotte's other brothers, who were in a tree being Spider-Man, and started back to Markham Street. On the way Daniel mentioned what he had really wanted to talk about all the time.

'Oh, by the way,' he said, trying to sound off-hand, 'I saw something weird when they were taking out the last thing.'

Charlotte knew Daniel very well and off-hand didn't work on her.

She stopped at once and turned to face him. 'What? Tell me.'

So he told her. When he had finished she didn't do any of the 'how can you be sure?' stuff he had been dreading. She just said, 'If it's a . . . you know . . . that would certainly be as good as anything – Romany, dogs, anything.'

Five
Percy

The next day when Daniel came home from school, their new neighbours had arrived. They were called Mr and Mrs Bosse-Lynch, and Great-Aunt Joyce, who had been spying from her window all day, was very satisfied. They had the right sort of car, and the right sort of clothes, and Mr Bosse-Lynch had started trimming the hedge immediately. Then two ladies from the town had arrived to clean the house, and Great-Aunt Joyce had heard Mrs Bosse-Lynch telling them what to do before they had even got through the door.

That night, when Daniel had put his light out and lay in the darkness waiting for sleep, he heard something. At first he thought that it must be a pigeon under the slates. But it wasn't the right cooing and scratching noise that pigeons made. It seemed to be coming from the wall beside his bed. On the other side of the wall, he knew, was an attic room just like his in the house next door. The noise was more a snuffling or gulping kind of noise. He sat up and put his ear to the wall. Now he could hear quite clearly. He heard stifled sobs, and sniffs. Someone was crying.

Daniel lay down again and tried to think. Perhaps Mrs Bosse-Lynch was secretly a very tragic person, with a horrible sad secret that she crept up to the attic and cried about at night. He hoped not, because he didn't want to feel sorry for someone whom Great-Aunt Joyce approved of. But it was far more likely that they had a prisoner in the attic. They had kidnapped someone, probably a rich man's daughter, and sneaked her into the house. Soon they would cut off her ear and send it to the desperate parents. On the other hand, it could be a poor mad relation whom they didn't want anybody to know about. Charlotte had read a book about someone like that. It was called *Jane Eyre* and was one of her absolute favourites.

Either way, Daniel had to make contact. He sat up again and knocked three times on the wall. The sniffling stopped.

'Hello, who's there?' he called. 'Do you need help?'

Still there was no sound. But then part of the wall slowly went soft and bulgy. The bulge got bigger, and separated itself from the wall. It was swirly and colourless, almost transparent. Then parts of it started taking shape, a hand appeared here, a leg there. The air in the room was suddenly icy cold, and in front of Daniel stood a small boy in a nightshirt, with golden curls and big weepy eyes.

'You are a ghost, aren't you?' said Daniel. 'I thought you were someone in trouble.'

'I am someone in trouble,' said the ghost, and huge ghostly tears started to roll down its cheeks. 'I am someone in terrible trouble.'

'I think I saw when you came,' said Daniel. 'You were in the removal van.'

'Yes, I was,' said the ghost. 'It wasn't a bus.' The tears rolled ever faster down its pale cheeks.

'Of course it wasn't a bus, it was a removal van.'

41

'But I thought it was,' gulped the ghost. 'And I don't know where I am and I don't know where Father and Mother are and—'

'Please try to stop crying,' said Daniel. 'And keep your voice down or you'll wake Great-Aunt Joyce.'

The ghost was obviously a young child, and seemed to be working himself into hysterics. 'If you calm down and tell me about it, I might be able to help.'

Daniel was secretly a bit disappointed. Ever since the arrival of the removal van he had been hoping for something really shockingly ghastly, perhaps a leering headless skeleton or a viciously grinning ghost murderer who dissolved his victims in acid. Anything really that would scare Great-Aunt Joyce to death, or at least make her flee from Markham Street and never return. But if she came up now and saw this weeping boy, she would probably just slap him and shoo him out.

However, even a small sad ghost is better than no ghost at all, and Daniel was a kind person and more than willing to sort out his problems if he could.

'You'd better tell me the whole story,' he said, and Perceval, for that was his name, came and sat on the bed and began.

Percy told his story with lots of pauses for miserable sniffing and cries of 'Oh, what am I to do?' and 'I shall be alone forever!', so it took him quite a long time.

Ronald and Iphigenia and Percy had materialized in good time at the service station, where they had met up with Cousin Vera and the other ghosts and spectres who had applied for Mountwood. There was

42

quite a crowd milling about the parking bay where the bus was to pick them up. Some of them were old acquaintances, and they hung about, chatting, catching up on each other's news. After a while, when the bus still hadn't come, Percy had got bored and wandered off. There were lots of great big lorries standing silent and dark in the parking area. Percy glided among them, peeping in sometimes to look at the drivers snoring in their cabs. They had little beds with curtains, which reminded Percy of when he had been alive and his mother had read poetry to him before he went to sleep. His favourite one had started, 'Where the bee sucks there suck I.'

When Percy got back to the pick-up place, he saw a bus standing in the parking bay, revving its engine. There were no ghosts to be seen. He cried, 'Help, help, wait for me! Don't leave without me!' and threw himself through the side of the bus just as it drew away and rumbled off into the night.

'But it wasn't a bus,' said Percy sadly, looking with at Daniel with tragic eyes. 'The bus had already left.'

'Well, why didn't your parents wait for you? They must have been worried sick when you didn't show up.'

'I don't know, I don't know. I have been aba . . . adn . . .'

'Abandoned.'

'Y-y-yes. Like the Babes in the Wood.' Percy collapsed in hopeless weeping.

When he had recovered slightly Daniel said, 'I still don't see how you could mistake a removal van for a bus.'

'But I've never *been* on a bus. And it had words on

the side like where we were going.'

'What do you mean?'

But Percy could speak no more. With a final wail of 'Poor me! Oh, sad unhappy me!' he threw himself face down on the bed.

Daniel heard Great-Aunt Joyce's bedroom door opening, and her tread on the stair.

'That's done it,' he said.

'I'll disappear,' said Percy. 'I'm quite good at it.' And he started to fade, vanishing just as Great-Aunt Joyce appeared in the doorway.

Daniel turned on his bedside light. Great-Aunt Joyce was wearing a flannel dressing gown and tartan slippers, and her hair was in curlers. She looked very angry, and peered around the room.

'Really, Daniel, this is appalling. What on earth is going on? I must have silence after my pill. I shall be speaking to your father.'

'Oh, it's you, Great-Aunt Joyce. I was having a terrible nightmare.'

'Were you now?' said Great-Aunt Joyce suspiciously, and it seemed to Daniel that she stared intently at the exact spot where Percy had just vanished. 'A nightmare, was it? That's what comes of not chewing your food properly. Poor digestion.'

When she had gone, a small voice spoke from the empty bed.

'She doesn't seem very nice,' said Percy.

'She isn't. We'll have to be absolutely quiet now, Percy. We'll talk about this tomorrow.'

Six
Mountwood

Percy's parents hadn't abandoned him. They would never do a thing like that. But when the ghost bus finally arrived there was quite a lot of confusion. It is always the same when people, or ghosts, are getting on a bus; there is quite a lot of pushing and shoving. Some of the ghosts were worried about travel sickness and wanted to be sure of a seat near the front; others wanted to sit with their friends, or bag a window seat. Ghosts are invisible a lot of the time, and sometimes as many as four or five ghosts tried to get in to the same seat. So it took quite a long time before they were all sorted out, and by that time the bus was well on its way, rushing north through the night.

The bus was old, and so was the driver. In fact both bus and driver had passed away many years before, when an unfortunate combination of too much beer and a sudden downpour had put an end to them at the bottom of an old quarry in the Peak District. It was quite surprising how fast the rusty old wreck with its mouldy seats and shattered windows could go, considering the crumpled mess that had once been its engine. But it was powered by something quite different from diesel fuel, and could even take cross-country short cuts if necessary.

'Where is Percy sitting?' said Iphigenia, when she had finally managed to persuade a pair of rather silly water-sprites to move from the seat next to her husband.

'I should think he is up at the front somewhere, near the driver. You know how he was looking forward to it.'

But when Iphigenia glided up the aisle a little later to see that he was all right, he wasn't there. She found Cousin Vera though, squashed into a window seat near the front beside a hugely fat ghost who had been housemaster at a famous public school and had died of apoplexy while enthusiastically thrashing a small pupil.

'Vera, darling, where is Percy sitting?' she asked.

'Oh, I thought he was with you,' said Vera.

Iphigenia, getting worried now, glided up and down the bus, calling for her son, but it was soon quite clear that Percy was not on board.

'Ronald, Percy is not here! Oh, my poor boy! We must make them turn round and go back.'

They went to talk to the driver.

'You must turn around immediately; our son has been left behind,' said Ronald.

'Can't do that,' said the driver. 'Can't mess up my schedule. Got a pick-up in Birmingham, and have to be at Mountwood before dawn. They were very clear about that, and I'm not going to get myself into trouble with those three.' He shivered, remembering his meeting with the three Great Hagges.

'But good grief, man, this is an emergency. Our son is lost.'

'Tell you what – I'll try to send a message to a mate of mine who haunts the service station. He'll find the boy and see he's all right until you can pick him up, or get him on to another bus.'

There was nothing to be done. Ronald fumed, Iphigenia pleaded and wept, but the driver was adamant. He wasn't turning back for a slip of a boy who'd missed the bus. The other passengers were sympathetic. Cousin Vera wailed, the other ghosts gnashed their teeth, rattled their chains, moaned and groaned as best they could, but it was no good.

In Birmingham the bus swooshed to a halt behind a disused gasworks in order to pick up a ghost called the Phantom Welder, who got on board with his phantom welding torch all a-sizzle and greeted his fellow-passengers with a cheery 'Mornin' everybody!'

He soon realized that the atmosphere on the bus was not a happy one.

Before they set off again the driver came down the aisle to talk to Ronald and Iphigenia.

'Well, I've got hold of my mate, and he's done a thorough search of the whole place, and your boy's not there. He's sure of it.'

'What? It's impossible!'

'That's what he said. Look, he's a ghost, isn't he? How bad can it be?'

'Oh, you foolish man!' cried Iphigenia. 'My little Percy is sensitive. He has an artistic soul. He is not just any boy. He will waste away in sorrow.'

But now Ronald sided with the driver. 'Perhaps we'd better calm down a bit, Iffy my dear. It might do the lad a bit of good to fend for himself for a while. Learn something about survival.'

'That's right,' said the driver. 'When we get to Mountwood the Great Hagges can put out a proper "Missing Ghost" alert, and he'll show up in no time.'

47

So the bus flew on towards its destination. But there was no denying that the passengers were a lot less chatty than they had been when they left. The Phantom Welder, who was a good-natured ghost in a boiler suit and liked to get a party going, tried to start a sing-song. But it fizzled out like a damp squib. Soon his welding torch fizzled out too, and the busload of ghosts travelled on in silence.

The bus drew to a halt in the front courtyard at Mountwood and the ghosts streamed out. Goneril was waiting to receive them.

'Welcome to Mountwood,' she declared. 'You are of course tired after your journey, but before you retire for the day, we would like you to join us for a short introduction in the assembly hall.'

She led the ghosts into the stone-flagged lower chamber of Mountwood, which was empty apart from three chairs on a raised dais. The Hagges had removed the cover from the well in the centre, so that Angus Crawe, who was after all the oldest inhabitant of Mountwood, could feel a part of things. So far he had kept himself to himself.

There were no chairs for the ghosts, because ghosts really have no need of chairs, except for the sheer fun of sitting in them, and as Drusilla had pointed out when they were arranging things, they weren't there to have fun. Fredegonda was sitting on the middle chair, with Drusilla to her left, and as Goneril took her place in the third chair, Fredegonda rose to speak.

She had made a real effort with her appearance.

'Correct, but not too formal, I think,' had been Drusilla's advice. So she had applied a bit of lipstick.

She had also found some horse-leeches in a pond behind the house and placed them in a circle round her throat, where they now hung, plump and glistening and looking very fetching.

Fredegonda smiled, and the effect, thanks to her bright green lipstick, was rather like slicing open a large watermelon. She began to speak. She was used to public speaking, and her voice carried easily to the back of the hall. In fact it carried all the way to the pub in the nearby village, where an old hill shepherd was nursing his evening pint. He shook his head. 'Those weather forecasts are blooming useless. Didn't say anything about thunderstorms.'

Fredegonda's speech was masterful. She told the ghosts about the great future that awaited them, about the satisfaction that hard work would bring and about all pulling together in a true spirit of fellowship. She said that there was no success without struggle, and no 'I' in 'team'. She made some little jokes to make everybody feel at home and she finished with a rousing cry: 'Ghosts of the world, unite! You have everything to win with your chains!'

But in spite of her magnificent oratory, Fredegonda felt that her speech had fallen a bit flat. She had not grabbed her audience by the throat. They had not hung on her every word. Some of the ghosts were only half there, or in some cases even less, just an eyeball or an elbow. Hardly any of them were completely visible. There was one couple in particular whom she noticed. The gentleman with no skin was obviously trying to stay in shape, but his wife just disappeared.

Afterwards the Great Hagges met in the staffroom for tea and titbits. Goneril came last. 'Sorry I'm late,' she said. 'I've been sorting out the dorms. Actually I'm rather disappointed. First day of school, you know, one expects a bit of chatter and larking about, but these are a glum lot. Apparently that married couple –' she consulted her list – 'Ronald and Iphigenia Peabody, managed to mislay their son, just a little chap. They're all in a state about it.'

'To be perfectly honest that's a bit of a relief,' said Fredegonda, 'I thought I was losing my touch. Getting rusty.'

'Oh no, it was a marvellous speech,' said Drusilla kindly, 'but we must put out a "Missing Ghost" alert straight away. We can't have something like that affecting their work.'

'I'll see to it,' said Goneril as she poured the tea, and they all tucked into the tasty worm tartlets, lightly dusted with dandruff, which Drusilla had prepared earlier.

Seven
Charlotte's Quest

When Daniel woke the following morning, Percy was nowhere to be found. He called out to him softly several times, but there was no reply. As soon as he could get away from the house, he went to look for Charlotte.

She lived at number two. He rang the bell, and Charlotte's mother came to the door carrying Charlotte's little sister, who had obviously been having her breakfast. A lot of it was on her face, and the rest of it seemed to be on Charlotte's mother.

'She's over at Mrs Wilder's, I think. Could you ask her to come back as soon as possible? I have to get up to the shops.'

Mrs Wilder lived at number eight, all alone in the house. Charlotte was there quite often, helping her. She would have helped even if Mrs Wilder hadn't had a house full of books and pictures, and a head full of interesting thoughts and memories, but it certainly made helping her more fun.

The door was open, and Daniel went into the hall and called up the stairs. 'Hello, Mrs Wilder. Is Charlotte there?'

'I'm up here,' came Charlotte's voice.

Mrs Wilder was getting pretty deaf. Daniel went up and put his head around the door of the big room on the first floor. It was the same kind of room as

51

Aunt Joyce's, at least in size and shape. But otherwise it was completely different. There were bookshelves packed with books, and a writing desk covered in notebooks and pens and papers, and pictures on the wall. On the old marble mantelpiece were all the usual things – photographs and invitations and a couple of candlesticks – and also some less usual things: a pack of hand-painted tarot cards, a badger's skull, a small silver coin from Afghanistan stamped with the head of Alexander.

In the corner of the room was something that might have been just an ordinary stick, but was in fact a blowpipe from an Amazonian tribe called the Wai-wai.

'A blowpipe is a marvellous murder weapon,' Mrs Wilder had told Daniel once when he had asked about it. 'Silent, deadly, accurate. And the poisons they use in South America kill in seconds.'

Mrs Wilder was a writer. She wrote detective stories and was quite famous. Now she was sitting at her desk, a small slim old lady with grey hair that kept escaping from her various pins and hairclips. You always noticed her eyes first. They were dark brown and looked at you as though they didn't see the outside of you at all, but saw everything that was going on inside your head. Her faced was lined – she was eighty-three. There were lines for smiling with, lines for crying with and lots of lines for thinking with.

Charlotte was sitting on the floor in the middle of the room, surrounded by an ocean of photographs, old and new.

'Hello, Daniel,' said Mrs Wilder. 'Charlotte is going

through the photo box. It's time to get it sorted. Soon it will be too late.'

Mrs Wilder was expecting to die any day now. She had been expecting it for years, but so far, apart from the usual difficulties of being eighty-three, she was very much alive.

'Charlotte, I have to talk to you,' said Daniel.

Charlotte looked at him. 'Is it what we were talking about?'

'Yes, but there's more to it.'

'How do you mean?'

Mrs Wilder understood immediately that they had something secret to discuss. 'Why don't you two go down to the kitchen and make me some coffee?' she said, and Daniel and Charlotte went downstairs.

'It was a ghost, and I've met him,' said Daniel, and while they made coffee and put Mrs Wilder's favourite biscuits on a plate, he told her all about it.

'We have to help him,' said Daniel when he had finished. 'I promised last night.'

'When can I meet him?'

'Come over tonight. I don't think he can appear in the daytime. He wasn't there this morning.'

After supper Charlotte went round to Daniel's house.

'Oh, hello, dear,' said Daniel's mother when she came to the door. 'Daniel said you would be coming over. You were going to help him with something.'

'That's right, Mrs Salter.' Charlotte didn't like lying – she thought it was weak – so she was glad that Daniel's mother didn't ask what Daniel needed help with. They had decided that grown-ups should be kept out of the whole thing for as long as possible.

Charlotte ran up the stairs to Daniel's room. They sat side by side on Daniel's bed.

'Percy, please appear now, we need to talk,' called Daniel softly.

Nothing happened. They could hear Great-Aunt Joyce thumping around in the room below. Then she too went quiet.

'Percy, please.' Daniel looked at Charlotte. 'He was here last night, I talked to him, I really did.'

'Of course you did; don't be stupid. There could be a thousand reasons why he doesn't answer. He might be asleep for all we know.'

'Do ghosts sleep?'

'Haven't the foggiest.'

'Let's turn the light out and just wait.'

They waited in the darkness for what seemed like a very long time. Charlotte began to think that she should be getting back, and wondered how she could tell Daniel in the right way, so that he wouldn't think she didn't believe in his ghost.

Then, just like the first time, a cold bluish bulge separated itself from the wall, and Percy appeared. He wasn't crying any more, but he looked miserable enough, standing there thin and semi-transparent in his nightshirt.

'How do you do?' said Charlotte. 'I'm Charlotte Hamilton.'

'I'm Perceval. Are you a girl?' Percy had lived in a time when no girl ever wore jeans and a T-shirt, so he wasn't quite sure.

'Yes, I am.'

'Do not fear.'

'That's all right, I'm not in the least frightened,' said Charlotte, and she could have kicked herself, because Percy started to wail.

'Oh, miserable failure that I am! No one fears me, not even girls.'

This got Charlotte very annoyed indeed, but she bit her lip this time, realizing that he had had a very old-fashioned upbringing which she would have to deal with later.

'Perhaps it's a good thing that we aren't terrified,' she said gently, 'because we want to help you find your parents.'

Daniel and Charlotte took it in turns to ask Percy questions that might give them some kind of a clue, but they didn't get much out of him.

He knew that it was a long journey to a special school for ghosts, and that it was in the country and had a name that sounded like the words on the removal van – 'Forest' and 'Hills'.

'Do you know what direction the school was in?' asked Daniel. 'North, south, east, west? I mean, it could be anywhere.'

'North,' said Percy. And however much they begged him to rack his brains, he had no more to add.

'Well, north is good,' said Charlotte. 'We're in the north.'

'Are we? Are we really?' Percy looked happy for the first time since they had met him. 'Can we go there now? I want to go now!'

But of course they had to disappoint him. Then north of England is big, and as Daniel said, there were probably loads of places that would fit the bill, with names like Woody Knoll or Cragtrees.

'I'm sorry, Percy, but we must do some research,' said Charlotte. 'Please don't cry again,' she added, as the little ghost's eyes filled once more with tears. 'We won't give up, you know. We will bring you to your parents. It's like a quest. Do you know what that is?'

Percy did know. 'My name comes from a quest,' he said, cheering up again. 'That's what Mother says.'

'Exactly. This is the quest of Perceval, and your parents are the grail.'

Daniel shook his head in amazement. 'Where do you get everything from?'

'Oh, come on, Daniel, the Legend of the Grail? Give me a break.'

Daniel's mother called from downstairs. 'I think you'd better be heading home now, Charlotte.'

'On my way, Mrs S.,' called Charlotte. 'Goodbye, Percy. Same time tomorrow, and we'll see if we have news for you.' And she went.

'I think she might find them,' said Percy. 'She seems jolly clever for a girl.'

'Yes, but don't ever say that to her. I mean it.'

Charlotte rang the next afternoon. 'Daniel, I'm at Mrs Wilder's again, can you come over?'

'You sound pleased with yourself.'

'I think we've found it.'

'We?'

'Just come over, will you?'

Charlotte answered the door, and they went upstairs to the big room, where Mrs Wilder was sitting

56

on her comfortable sofa, reading the newspaper.

'Hello, Daniel,' she said. 'Don't tell Charlotte off. I was curious and I got it out of her.'

'You see,' said Charlotte, 'it's like a crossword clue: "*Forest and Hills, school in the north*". And so of course I thought of coming here.'

Mrs Wilder did a lot of crosswords, even very difficult ones.

'I tried to lie about it, but it didn't come off.'

'You'd better leave the lying to me in future,' said Daniel. 'You're absolutely pathetic at it.'

'You won't tell, will you?' he asked Mrs Wilder. 'I think my parents have enough to deal with at the moment.'

'My dear Daniel,' said Mrs Wilder in a very dignified voice, 'I am perfectly aware that this is confidential information.'

'And you believe us, don't you?'

'Heavens above! One more ghost is neither here nor there to me,' she replied, and her gaze drifted off for a moment, back down the long years.

'Well,' said Charlotte, 'a school for ghosts has to be a big place, doesn't it? And you can't have it in the middle of a town. So that means somewhere out in the country. But there are an awful lot of big estates in the borders; I had no idea. Most of them are occupied though, or have been turned into hotels and conferences centres and so on. Then Mrs Wilder was absolutely brilliant; it must be because of writing detective stories.'

'Fairly brilliant, I think it's fair to say,' said Mrs Wilder, looking up from her paper.

'No, *really* brilliant,' said Charlotte. She went on.

'Mrs Wilder said that if the school had only just been started, then maybe some place had been rented out or bought quite recently, just a month or two ago. So we started calling all the estate agents in the north of England, but there was nothing even remotely like "Forest and Hills". I was ready to give up, and then Mrs Wilder was brilliant again.'

'Twice in one morning,' muttered Mrs Wilder. 'Not bad for an ancient person.'

'She said that the agent might be across the border,' said Charlotte, 'so we started on Scotland. Then we got lucky. Someone gave us the number of a big firm in Edinburgh that handles the sale of large properties. It was odd really. When I rang and asked if there had been a recent sale in the borders, perhaps to some retired ladies – you remember Percy called them Great Hagges, but I couldn't say that – then the man I was talking to started babbling and saying that everything was in order, and if it wasn't he would see to it immediately and please don't let them come back. I got the name out of him though: Mountwood.' She looked triumphantly at Daniel.

'And look at this,' she went on. 'Mrs Wilder said she had an old book somewhere about big houses of the borders, and she dug it out.'

She pointed at the book that lay open on Mrs Wilder's desk, and Daniel saw an old photograph of a rather forbidding fortified manor house, surrounded by dark crags and fir trees. The caption read 'Mountwood, ancestral home of one of the fiercest clan chiefs of the borders.'

Daniel almost shouted. 'You've found it! It has to be the place! That's amazing!'

Charlotte and Mrs Wilder looked very pleased with themselves.

Then Daniel said more soberly, 'Now all we have to do is get Percy there.'

Eight
Journey by Moonlight

The Stinking Druid of Llwnannog occupied a single room at Mountwood. He was a tall thin ghost, and everything about him was a dirty greyish white – his shoulder-length straggly hair, his trailing robes, his bushy eyebrows and his long horse-like face.

When Goneril was making her list of who would stay where, she hadn't found anyone who wanted to be his room-mate. All the other ghosts had made some kind of excuse. It wasn't because of his disgusting stench; ghosts don't have human noses; their senses are of a different sort. It was because he knew all the ancient lays of the Celtic mysteries off by heart, some of which had thousands of verses, and he never recited just a part, but always a whole one.

The Druid didn't mind being on his own, not really. He was used to it, and even when he was alive in Wales more than two thousand years ago, he hadn't had any special friends. Now he watched dreamily from the little mullioned window of his room as a huge pale moon freed itself from a tangle of dark branches to sail the night sky. He thought of many things, but mostly he thought of the lovely maiden who was the only person who ever truly understood him, and how he had loved her, and how she had caused him to sin. He had saved her from being burned in a wicker basket at the Great

Festival of Beltane, on Mayday eve.

As a Druid, a member of the ancient Celtic priesthood, he was all in favour of human sacrifices in principle. But he had been so very attached to the girl. It was a terrible thing to do, to secretly exchange her, the Chosen One, for one of his aunts whom he particularly disliked. He almost got away with it, but the Chosen One had been discovered, alive and well, in the hollow oak where he had hidden her, and it all came out. The Chief Druid had been absolutely livid and had cursed him horribly so that he was doomed to wander for eternity, with the smell as a special punishment. He had disliked his aunt because she had made him cut her toenails when he was a boy, and she had very smelly feet.

'Smelly she was, and smelly shalt thou be,' the Chief Druid had intoned.

The Stinking Druid sighed. If he hadn't sinned, he would have been one of the famous Nine Standing Men of Llwnannog, those great stones standing peacefully and odour-free on the hill above the village, visited by bus-loads of American and Japanese tourists every summer. That would really be something. Every year hundreds of tourists asked why there were only eight stones, when they were called the Nine. Nobody knew, but he knew.

The Druid's thoughts turned to Mountwood, and his secret hope. If he did really well, then perhaps the curse would be lifted. He wasn't up to much, he was aware of that. He had signed up for extra lessons in Gnashing of Teeth, but he was having a hard time of it. It isn't easy to gnash when you only have one tooth. But he was determined to work really hard, and he would do his exercises, and perhaps, one day, he would be forgiven.

From the courtyard below came a mournful howl. 'Oh dear, I'm late,' said the Druid. 'They've started the voice class without me.'

Just as he was about to leave his place at the window and float downstairs, he saw two small figures approaching the house, walking down the track from the main road. There was enough moonlight for him to see that they were children, living ones. The boy had a rucksack, and they walked slowly, as though they were tired.

Daniel and Charlotte *were* tired. In fact they were exhausted. Mountwood was not easy to get at – they had soon found that out when they started looking at timetables and making plans.

It wasn't too difficult to get to Carlisle, which had a train service. But then they had to get a bus, then another bus, and finally, in the late afternoon, they got off at a small village and still had quite a way to go. They had decided to use the rest of their money to take a taxi the last bit, even though it meant no supper and nothing to eat on the return journey. They rang the number that was posted on the bus shelter, and the man who answered sounded cheerful enough and said he would be there in five minutes, after he had drunk his tea.

'Where are you going then?' he asked.

'To Mountwood.'

There was silence at the other end. Then, 'Look, sorry, I've got another job. Forgot all about it. I can't help you.'

'But we don't mind waiting.'

'It's a long job. Won't be back till after midnight.'

'Is there anyone else who could take us?'

'Not in this village. What do you want to go there for anyway?'

'It's part of a school project.'

'Do your project somewhere else, if you've got any sense.' And he hung up.

There was nothing for it but to walk.

The first mile went well enough. As the light faded and the shadows lengthened Percy appeared faintly beside them, chattering away about the buses and the train they had travelled on. He was already feeling much more grown-up and couldn't understand how he had mistaken a removal van for a bus.

'Oh, what a lot I shall have to tell Mother and Father!' he said excitedly.

The further they walked, and the later it got, the more cheerful Percy became. Of course for a ghost the night is the time to be up and about, whereas Charlotte and Daniel were almost asleep on their feet.

'Can we go faster? I want to get there soon,' said Percy.

'No, we can't. In fact I need a rest,' said Charlotte. She sat down at the side of the road with her back against a drystone wall. It had been particularly hard for her, making up a story to tell her mother. She would have her hands full the whole weekend with the children, and no one to help her. They had told some silly story about a school project on castles and spending the night with a friend who had moved to Carlisle. Charlotte had hated having to do that. Now the sun was setting, they had miles to go and she was dog-tired.

'I suppose we'd better wait a bit then,' said Percy. 'You're probably not very strong, you're only a g—'

'Percy!' Daniel almost shouted. 'Now you shut your mouth, and keep it shut.'

Percy vanished.

'You've hurt his feelings, Daniel,' said Charlotte. 'He's only a little kid.'

'Stuff him,' said Daniel. 'He's a pain in the neck. The sooner we get shot of him the better. A ghost who's too scared to scare people, I mean, honestly.'

They went on. A big fat moon rose over the moor.

At last they found the turning and trudged down the eerily moonlit track towards the dark building that loomed at the end of the valley.

'This should be the place,' said Charlotte. 'It's certainly creepy enough.'

It was a bit unnerving walking into that dark valley, where the fir trees cast inky-black moon shadows and strange rustles and squeaks could be heard from the grasses and bracken that lined the track. Percy did not reappear, although Daniel called out and apologized for shouting at him. The little ghost seemed to be still in a sulk, and Daniel and Charlotte began to wish he was around to give them an introduction when they arrived. They were not the kind of children who got all hysterical about just any ghost, but they knew that there were things in the invisible world that were a lot nastier than Percy, and if he wasn't with them, they might not be very welcome.

Goneril was in charge of the evening session. It was not going well. The students had been at Mountwood for almost a week, and they seemed to be making no progress at all. They made heavy weather of even the simplest exercises, basic stuff like materialization and sudden scary noises. Class discipline was lax to say the least. The Phantom Welder had decided to be the clown of the group and cracked stupid jokes that made the sprites titter. The Stinking Druid was so unhappy and unsure of himself that he just stood at the back and sighed, and this evening he hadn't even turned up. But worst of all were the couple who had mislaid their son; they were so droopy and half-hearted that they were driving Goneril mad. She had had great hopes for them. She was an experienced judge of these things, and could tell that Iphigenia was a skilful professional at heart, and Ronald a real worker. It is very upsetting for any teacher when pupils simply cannot or will not make the best of themselves.

'Please, Mrs Peabody, could you try to put a bit more energy into the moaning. We are looking for the hair-raising effect,' said Goneril.

But it was no good. Iphigenia came to the front of the class and produced a weary whimper which would not have raised a single hair on the head of a nervous five-year-old.

Then a foul stench filled the air, and the Stinking Druid appeared. But instead of sneaking in at the back of the class as he usually did, he glided forward and spoke.

'Excuse me, Miss Goneril, but I think we have visitors.'

At that moment the front doorbell rang, a loud clanging that echoed through the castle. All the ghosts instantly vanished.

'What on earth . . . ?' said Goneril, and strode to the foot of the stairs.

'Fredegonda, Drusilla,' she called, 'there's someone at the door. I think we should deal with it.'

Daniel and Charlotte stood before the great door of Mountwood and listened to the fading echoes of the bell. They were cold, tired, and more than a little uneasy. The castle seemed to be completely deserted.

'If we are wrong, and the place is empty, then we are in for a rough night,' said Daniel.

'And even if it isn't empty . . .' Charlotte replied.

'It isn't,' said Daniel, and Charlotte too heard the sound of heavy footsteps approaching.

The door creaked slowly open and three extremely large ladies stood looking down at them.

'Children!' exclaimed the middle one.

'What are you doing here? At this time of night?' asked the one on the left.

'Are you lost?' asked the third.

'Er . . . er . . .' said Daniel.

'Speak up, boy. Has the cat got your tongue?' thundered Fredegonda.

Charlotte found her voice. 'Sorry to bother you, but we are looking for the Great Hagges of Mountwood.'

'The what? Pure gibberish,' rasped Goneril. 'We are simply three pensioners who have no wish to be disturbed by little brats. We were just on our way to bed.'

'But . . .' stuttered Daniel.

Before he could say more a small clear voice rang out. 'Mother, Father, I'm here, I'm back. I was in a removal van but now I'm here. I've been on a bus, and on a train.'

The next half-hour or so was one that Daniel and Charlotte would never forget. A spectral light filled the courtyard and ghosts of all shapes and sizes started to appear around them, screeching, wailing, waving ghostly limbs about and then putting them back on again. Severed heads bobbed about, bleeding happily and smiling like idiots.

In the midst of the crowd, as though in a private place of their own, Iphigenia stood hugging Percy to her breast, while Ronald stood and patted him on the head and said in a voice filled with fatherly pride and love, 'Well done, lad, what a boy you are, you made it, a chip off the old block.'

Daniel and Charlotte were forgotten. They sat down a bit out of the way, with their backs to the wall of the castle, partly because it is a bit odd having ghosts passing through you all the time, and partly because the Stinking Druid had joined the happy throng and neither of them wanted to vomit in front of the Great Hagges.

At last Fredegonda, in a voice like the foghorn of an ocean liner, brought the joyful crowd to their senses.

'Enough!' she roared. The ghosts started to quieten down. Fredegonda stepped up to Percy, who looked up at her shyly.

'Well, you seem to have been found. I presume our Missing Ghost alert got through to someone.'

'No, Miss Hagge,' said Percy. 'I don't know about that. It was them. It was Daniel and Charlotte who helped me,' and he pointed at the two children sitting quietly by the wall.

'They're the best friends ever.'

'Humans?' Fredegonda's voice was terrible. 'You were helped by humans? You are FRIENDS with HUMAN BEINGS?'

'Bleeding 'eck,' whispered the Phantom Welder to himself. 'That's torn it.'

Fredegonda marched towards the children, who scrambled to their feet. Daniel found himself smoothing down his hair. Charlotte tried to brush a bit of the dirt off the front of her jeans.

The Great Hagge towered above them, arms akimbo and a fierce glitter in her eye.

'You are mere chits, sprogs. You are humans. You are no doubt terrified by what you have seen this night.'

'Well, a bit ... frightened,' said Charlotte. She didn't want to say that by far the scariest thing in that courtyard was the Great Hagge Fredegonda.

Fredegonda snorted. She turned and in a mighty voice addressed the assembled phantoms.

'Now, perhaps, you understand. These children, these weak and tiny things, are *a bit frightened*. They are not petrified, or horror-struck. They have not been driven mad with fear, or died of sheer terror. Their hair has not turned white, they do not even tremble. It is not good enough; it will not do. You have brought shame upon the name of true haunting. You must apply yourselves to your work unceasingly and put this failure behind you. And until then it is absolutely against school rules to have any communication, friendly or otherwise, with members of the human race. Now please disappear. There will be no more lessons tonight.'

Within seconds the courtyard was empty.

Now Fredegonda turned back to Daniel and Charlotte. 'As for you two, Goneril will run you into the village in the morning.' She turned away. 'Come, girls, I am calling an emergency staff meeting.'

The three Great Hagges stumped back into Mountwood, slamming the door behind them.

Daniel and Charlotte stood outside. It was cold, dark and damp.

'Rotten cow,' said Charlotte.

'Our French teacher is a bit like her,' said Daniel.

Then a voice whispered gently on the night air. 'I daren't appear, but I just had to thank you.'

It was Iphigenia. 'Percy has told me everything and, oh you darlings, I am so, so, grateful. I shall be in your debt until the end of time. If we can ever be of help . . . I shouldn't say that, should I . . . ? But I mean it, I do.'

There was a moment of silence, and then, very faintly, they heard, 'There is straw in the byre.' And Iphigenia was gone.

Daniel and Charlotte found the byre, an old stone building close by with a half-collapsed roof. Inside it was pitch dark, but they felt their way forward and burrowed into the heap of old straw that lay there. They crept close together for warmth, and fell into an exhausted sleep.

Afterwards Daniel thought that the most surprising part of their whole trip came the next morning, when they rode to the bus stop in the village in the back seat of a 1912 Rolls-Royce Silver Ghost driven by a Great Hagge called Goneril.

PART TWO

Nine
Jack Bluffit

Jack Bluffit, head of the city Department of Planning, stood gazing out of his office window. His office was right at the top of the council building, with one wall almost entirely made of glass, so the whole city was spread out below him. *His* city – that was how he thought of it. He had been born in it, grown up in it and seen it change. Lots of the changes were his work, planned by him, and he was proud of it. People moaned about old buildings and narrow streets being torn down to make way for shiny new tower blocks and big roads and flyovers; they whined about the city losing its 'character', or its 'charm'. Jack despised them. He knew better. He remembered well enough the slum where he was born. He remembered the miners with their sunken chests and the horrid coughs that would kill them. That was charm all right. He remembered his mother going out to scrub, and coming home exhausted with chapped hands, to put a meal of bread and dripping on the table. He remembered the earth closet at the back of the house which always stank. He remembered the kids with rickets and heads that had been shaved by the nit lady at school. That was character, was it?

Jack himself had no children; he had never wanted any. 'The city is my baby. I've given it the best years of my life,' he used to say, whenever some office worker started boring him to death about how their Sheila had got top marks in history or played 'Twinkle, Twinkle, Little Star' on the recorder. Children were just a waste of time and money, in Jack's view. Snot and nappies and expensive rubbishy toys that got broken the next day. He had more important things to do. He had been determined from the age of seven to make things change, and he had done it. It had been a long hard fight to the top. But now he was there. He was the strong man of the city. The politicians on the council came and went. Here one year, gone the next. Talking and voting. But Jack Bluffit was always there, making plans.

That's what he was doing now, as he gazed down on his city. From his window he could see the long sweep of the street that led down to the railway station, and halfway along was a great big monument, with a statue of Lord Lilford on it. Carved on the pediment was an inscription that Jack had read a thousand times on his way to the station. 'Lord Lilford, Benefactor of this City.' Now Jack saw in his mind's eye a bronze statue; a statue of a man seated on a powerful rearing horse, the great curve of its neck and the noble head reined effortlessly in by one firm hand. In the other hand, held aloft for all to see, was a roll of paper (bronze paper, of course): the plans for the regeneration of the city. And the proud determined face of the rider was the face of Jack Bluffit. He would have something better than children to remember him when he was gone, he would make sure of that. The city would remember him.

*

Jack went over to his desk and sat down. He leaned back in his chair and clasped his hands behind his head. The chair creaked and complained. Jack was no lightweight. He had thick hairy arms, a thick neck and a solid square head. He had a big round stomach which strained his shirt buttons, and big round thighs. He looked like the kind of person you might meet working on an offshore oil rig or a construction site. Sometimes people made the mistake of thinking that a thick body went with a thick head. But they usually regretted it. Jack could never have got where he was if he had been stupid. He was wily. Nothing got built or pulled down in the city without Jack Bluffit's say-so. He always got what he wanted, and he did not much care how. As far as Jack Bluffit was concerned, rules and regulations were only there to keep the little people in their place, and if they were stupid enough to let that happen, well, hard luck for them. When he narrowed his sharp little eyes and pursed his thick lips and started to work out ways of getting what he wanted, there were not many council workers or politicians who could stand in his way, and now there was something that Jack wanted very badly.

There were some unopened letters on his desk, and Jack started to look through them. Most of them were official business, but one was a card with stylish writing on it. 'Lord Ridget has the pleasure of inviting you to join the hunt at Ridget Hall on Sunday the 23rd . . .'

Jack Bluffit snorted. That snob Ridget would never have had him within fifty miles of Ridget Hall if he could help it. But Jack knew what he was after. Jack had plans that made Lord Ridget tremble in his posh shoes. If Ridget thought that he could twist his arm by impressing him with his snooty county friends, he had another think coming. But then something struck Jack. He would have to pose for the statue, and he had to look natural. He didn't want people snickering when it was unveiled and saying that he had never sat on a horse in his life. A bit of practice would come in handy. And it couldn't be that difficult. If that gangling chinless wonder Ridget could ride, then anybody could. He took a sheet of paper out of the desk drawer and wrote a reply.

There was a little knock at the door and it opened slowly. Bluffit's personal assistant slid into the room. He was thin and sharp-faced, very neatly dressed with short hair that seemed to be stuck to his head, and had a way of looking about him all the time as though he thought someone was spying on him.

'What?' barked Bluffit.

'Sorry to disturb you, Mr Bluffit, but you said I should let you know as soon as the decision came through.' He held out a folder with the city crest embossed on the front.

'Right, give it here then, and get out.'

His assistant slid out again, closing the door carefully behind him. Bluffit didn't like slammed doors, unless he was the one doing the slamming.

As soon as he had gone Bluffit opened the folder and leafed quickly through to the last page, which began, 'The motion to approve for development . . .' Then there was a long sentence which he skimmed through, looking for the words he wanted to see. There they were: '. . . has been passed.'

A satisfied smile spread over his features, but it didn't stay there very long. There was work to be done. He got up, opened the office door and yelled, 'Get in here!'

His assistant's name was Frederick Snyder, but Bluffit was a rude man. He called it being 'no-nonsense' and 'to the point', as rude people often do.

'Right,' he said, when Frederick was back in the room and standing in front of the desk. 'We're ready to go. The approval has come through.'

'Yes, sir.' Frederick knew already. He made it his business to know everything before anybody else.

'Get the announcement ready . . .'

'I've already done that, sir.' Frederick smirked. 'It will be in the papers this evening. If you approve, of course.' His eyes swivelled to the office door and back again to Bluffit. 'And the letters . . . ?' he said.

'Send them out right now, if not sooner. All the residents, the usual thing.'

'Of course, sir. Though I was just about to take my lunch break, sir.' But the look on Jack Bluffit's face made him decide not to take his lunch break after all.

When Frederick had removed himself Jack crossed to one of the filing cabinets that lined the opposite wall. He took out a rolled-up blueprint and flattened it out on his desk. He pored over it intently for a while, grunting with satisfaction. Yes, it looked good; the new bypass, the slip roads, the shopping centre – retail park, they called it – all laid out in detail. It would be a proper bit of modernization. Plenty of demolition to do first though. They would have to make a clean sweep of all those old houses. Tomorrow Bluffit would start making calls and lining up contractors.

He owed a favour or two. Jack reached for a felt-tip pen. His hand hovered over the blueprint and then descended decisively to place a red cross right in the middle, where the main entrance to the retail park would be.

'That's the spot,' said Jack.

Ten
Bad News

Sometimes after something really interesting has happened, life can seem a bit flat. Finding Mountwood and meeting the ghosts and the Hagges had been very interesting. Now life in Markham Street went on as usual, and there was nothing wrong with that, but there wasn't much for Daniel and Charlotte to get excited about, if you didn't count the end of term coming closer, and the summer holidays to look forward to. Tompkins disappeared, and everybody went looking for him, until he turned up in a suitcase on top of Mrs Cranford's wardrobe. And one of Charlotte's small brothers swallowed a goldfish, and had to be taken to the doctor's, not because of the goldfish, which as Charlotte pointed out was only a fish and people eat fish all the time, but because it had been dead and floating in the park lake, and could have had any number of germs.

Charlotte was pretty busy, either helping out at home or doing homework. She was absolutely determined to get top marks in everything. So on the days when only Great-Aunt Joyce would be at home, Daniel took to popping in after school to talk to Mr Jaros who lived at number four.

He was certainly interesting. He had a lot of white hair and a beaky nose with deep furrows on either side of it. He always wore a waistcoat and trousers that had once been part of a whole suit. But his old Labrador, Jessie, had lain down on the jacket one day when he had thrown it into a corner and, since she obviously liked it better than he did, he had let her keep it. Now he wore a pullover instead. He was a bow-maker, and he had his workshop on the ground floor. He didn't make bows for archery; he made bows for musical instruments, and as he often explained to Daniel it was a very highly skilled craft, and one which very few people understood.

In fact, he told Daniel, he was the best bow-maker in England, probably the best in Europe.

'Though I say it myself; I cannot hide myself from the truth. Compared to me, that man in Geneva is a pimple.'

He talked very precise English, far too well to really be English, which he wasn't. He had been born in Czechoslovakia, and had had some fairly nasty experiences there that he preferred not to talk about. 'What's done is done. What's past is past concern,' he used to say. He quite often sounded as though he was quoting something that he had read, which he often was.

Mr Jaros's workshop would have been a nice place to spend time even if Mr Jaros hadn't been there. There was a long workbench, and wood shavings on the floor, and on the wall hung the tools of his trade: chisels, knives, awls, dividers, clamps, pliers, tongs and files. There was a smell of resin, turpentine and pipe tobacco. There was a dusty CD player on a shelf, and something was almost always playing, mostly music by Smetana and Dvořák and Janáček, composers who, Mr Jaros maintained, were the greatest of them all. Bows of every description hung everywhere, small ones for children's first violins and great big ones for double basses, finished ones, half-finished ones and some that were only just started.

Mr Jaros had cleared a corner of the workbench and Daniel was making a birthday present for Charlotte, a box with a proper hinged lid where she could keep things. Mr Jaros had said that he would help Daniel put in a working lock with a key, so that whatever Charlotte decided to keep in there couldn't be eaten by her small brothers. And on the lid Daniel was going to carve her initials. He was using walnut wood, so it wasn't easy, with the hardness and the shortness of the fibres, and he had to use razor-sharp tools. Mr Jaros was strict, and Daniel had had to spend one whole afternoon learning to hone his chisels properly.

'A dull workman uses dull tools. If you take my edges off, you must put them back on.' Daniel was determined to do it right, with dovetail joints at the corners. So far he hadn't cut himself very badly, and Mr Jaros's sticking-plaster supplies had only been needed three or four times.

But the best thing about Mr Jaros's workshop was old Jessie, who lay and snored on her jacket in the corner for most of the day. She always opened one eye when Daniel came in and said hello to her, and she thumped her tail a couple of times. Daniel took her out for a walk sometimes, though she wasn't much of a walker these days.

'She runs in her sleep, and plays,' said Mr Jaros. 'Time can't take that away from her.'

But he knew that time would take her away from him soon enough, and he didn't like to think about that.

One day a few weeks after the trip to Mountwood, Daniel was at the workbench smoothing down the bevelled edge of his box and Mr Jaros was looking through a delivery of horsehair and complaining.

'Ah, there is no true quality to be had any more. If you could only have seen the pure-white perfect tails of the stallions of the Puszta.'

He went over to the little wood-burning stove that he had brought all the way from Prague in the boot of his car and poured out a coffee for himself from the ancient pot that was standing on it. He offered Daniel a ginger nut. Then the doorbell rang, and they heard the sound of letters being pushed through the letter box and landing on the hall floor.

'Do you mind, Daniel?'

Daniel went out. He came back and handed over the post. Mr Jaros took it and sorted through the bundle.

'It is so rarely interesting,' he said. 'I do not wish to have fun and sun in Ibiza, even if I should win the competition . . . but what have we here?'

He held up an official-looking envelope stamped with the town crest. 'Have they raised the rates again?'

He reached for a knife from the workbench and slit open the envelope. He took out the letter and read. Then he took off his glasses and walked over to the window. He stood for a long time, gazing silently out.

'Mr Jaros?' said Daniel. There must be something serious in the letter.

Mr Jaros turned round. The lines on either side of his nose seemed deeper than ever, and his dark eyes stared at Daniel, seeming to look right through him. Then he recovered himself.

'I think you should go home now, Daniel. That is enough for today.'

Then Daniel knew that something was very wrong. Mr Jaros had never told him to go home before.

Mrs Wilder looked down from the window of her big room on the first floor and saw her next-door neighbour Karin Hughes walking up the front path. The doorbell rang and then she heard Mrs Hughes in the hall.

'Hello, Lottie, are you in?'

'Of course I'm in, dear,' called Mrs Wilder. 'Come on up.'

'Shall I make us some tea first?'

'Please.'

'I won't be a minute.'

Karin Hughes was rather more than a minute, and when she came up carrying the tea tray she was wearing a slight frown, which she often wore when she had been in Mrs Wilder's kitchen.

It was many years now since Karin Lindblad, as she was then, had moved from her parents' farm in Sweden to England. She had got quite used to people walking straight into their houses without taking their shoes off (she had had bad nightmares about that in the beginning, after seeing what was on the city pavements). And when she had recovered from the shock of seeing fitted carpets in the toilet, and huge open fires that sucked all the heat out of the cold damp houses and straight up the chimney, she had got to work teaching her husband, who was an understanding man and loved her a lot, some simple things that even an imbecile could do, like taking your shoes off in the hall and bottling raspberry juice. In the few minutes she had spent in Mrs Wilder's kitchen she had dealt with most of the surfaces, sneaked some pots of home-made jam into the larder and done a bit of organizing. Karin Hughes had a deep respect for the mystery of writing, so she understood that Mrs Wilder was quite unlike ordinary people who saw things like mouse droppings where no mouse droppings should be.

'We have had a strange letter,' she said, putting down the tray and sitting down on the sofa. 'David is away, and I thought I would ask you about it.'

Mrs Wilder got up from her seat at the window and came to sit beside Karin on the sofa.

'One like this?' she asked, holding out her own letter.

'Yes, just the same. What is it all about?'

'This, Karin,' said Mrs Wilder quietly, 'is a Compulsory Purchase Order. They are going to pull down our houses and build a motorway.'

'But they can't. Not just like that.'

'They can, my dear. Oh yes, they can.'

'But where will we go?'

'They will give us money to go somewhere else. Compensation.'

'Money? Money? They will take my garden, my kitchen, my home, my neighbours. How will money help my heart-sorrow?' Sometimes when she was upset Mrs Hughes translated directly from her mother tongue, 'They cannot do this.'

'But they can, Karin,' said Mrs Wilder for the second time. And then again, 'They can.'

Eleven
The Shortener

'Things have certainly perked up a bit,' said Fredegonda.

Dawn was beginning to bathe the crag behind Mountwood in a rosy glow, and the Great Hagges were thinking about bed after a hard night's work. The students had dematerialized some time ago, but the Hagges had as usual stayed up to discuss the night's efforts.

'I'm very pleased to see that the Peabody couple have pulled their socks up,' Fredegonda went on.

It was true. Since the return of Percy to the bosom of his family all the ghosts had applied themselves to their work, but none more than Ron and Iphigenia, who clearly felt that they had some catching up to do. Only last night Ron had managed to materialize his lidless eyeballs all on their own, and made them revolve in different directions, so that you could see the muscles working. It really would have been terrifying if anybody in Mountwood, Hagge or ghost, had been able to be terrified. And Iphigenia had shown such skill in the voice-and-movement class that the Hagges were seriously considering using her as an assistant teacher for some of the serious remedial cases, such as Vera the Banshee, or the Druid.

'Though that tree-sprite's behaviour is really not acceptable,' said Goneril. 'I saw that you took her aside and had a word.'

'I most certainly did,' said Fredegonda. 'I think we will see some changes tomorrow.'

'You were being a bit unfair, you know,' said Drusilla. 'Some blame attaches to the Phantom Welder, you must admit.'

They were talking about an incident earlier that night, when the Druid had been asked to appear with his own heart pierced by a golden sickle and dripping blood. He had been extremely nervous about doing this in front of the whole class, and had released such a noisome stench that two bats that had been hanging from the roof beams fell stone dead into Drusilla's lap, and the kitten that Percy had found in the byre and was playing with in a corner lurched drunkenly across the room and toppled into the well, where it disturbed Angus Crawe with its yowling and had to be rescued with some difficulty.

As the revolting fumes had spread around the room, the Phantom Welder had whispered into the sprite's ear, 'Oops, been at the beans again,' and the silly thing had got one of those unstoppable fits of the giggles, which had reduced the Druid to tears. At least they thought that's what had happened. He certainly vanished and wild sobbing was heard.

'Perhaps I was a bit harsh,' said Fredegonda. 'The welder is terribly uncouth. But I fear that sprite encourages him.'

'Well, let's turn in,' said Goneril. 'Tomorrow is another night. And rather a special one. It's the dark of the moon, of course, and we have to start thinking about their individual projects, now that the basics are in place.'

'I've made us a hot drink,' said Drusilla. 'It's in the thermos on the bedside table.'

'My goodness, you do spoil us, Drusilla,' said Fredegonda, as they made their way to the bedroom.

'Not at all, you deserve it. And I simply had to use that gall bladder, you know. Waste not want not, as they say.'

The Great Hagges got ready for bed. Goneril took the most time about it, because she was a bit worried about the state of her knees. In her youth she had been very proud of them, with their scabby lumps and hairy moles, but recently she had thought they were looking rather smooth. Not quite like human knees, of course, but getting there. Drusilla had produced an ointment that she had made herself ('But don't ask what's in it, dear, it's an absolute secret'), and now Goneril applied it thoroughly.

'Oh, do hurry up,' said Fredegonda, who was already in her nightie. She swallowed the last of her drink and climbed into bed, followed by Drusilla. At last Goneril too was ready, and she joined them in the huge four-poster they shared. It had been there when they moved into Mountwood, but although built to take the weight of overfed clan chieftains and their companions, it had collapsed instantly when Goneril sat on it to try it out. However, a bit of work with some old oak beams had soon sorted that out. It wasn't very comfortable, but Great Hagges snort at comfort. In a surprisingly short time the massive structure was trembling and shaking with the huge snores of its occupants.

*

Meanwhile, elsewhere in the castle, the Shortener was having trouble achieving the peaceful state of almost non-existence that is the spectral version of sleep.

As the daylight grew stronger and the sun threatened to appear over the horizon, he tossed and turned, now invisible, now vaguely discernible, and simply could not find peace. He was doing fairly well on the course, he thought, but he couldn't shake off the horrible experience that had brought him there in the first place. It had shamed him; it was as simple as that.

His mind turned to the deserted chapel on its windswept promontory that was his home. Ghosts don't usually haunt churches or chapels or other places of worship, because the clergymen who are in charge of them are very particular about which other-worldly beings they are prepared to associate with, and they have quite effective methods – bells, books and candles to name but a few – of dealing with the ones they don't approve of. But no priest of any denomination had set foot in this chapel for years. In fact the place had been abandoned when the Shortener was still alive.

He remembered happy days working in his little funeral parlour among the coffins and corpses. He had always been a thrifty man, and had never understood why there was such a fuss about some simple adjustments that saved everybody time and expense. The removal of feet, or indeed sawing through shin bones in the case of particularly tall cadavers, meant much shorter coffins, and that was a saving of several pounds. The simple people of his village should have been grateful to him. But they weren't. The Shortener sighed. Instead, when they found his little cupboard with the extra parts in it, they had simply thrown him over the cliff without a second thought.

But that wasn't what caused him such pain; he had returned to haunt the chapel happily for many years. Then, only a month or two ago, a gang of teenagers had broken through one of the boarded-up windows and started malarkeying about among the pews. The girls had very short skirts and lots of make-up. The boys had baseball caps (although they never played baseball) and basketball shoes (although they never played basketball) and ripped jeans, although they weren't very poor and had hard-working parents, as far as he knew. The Shortener had seen his chance to give them a real fright, and waited patiently for a moment of silence, so that he could eerily appear and smile the little smile he had been practising. At last the moment came. But just as he was materializing behind the dusty altar, one of the boys said, 'Hey, check this out,' and they all rushed round to peer at something that glowed faintly bluish in his hand.

'Eeuu . . . that's disgusting!'

'Shift over and let me see . . .'

'That is *unreal* . . .'

They used a lot of other words that the Shortener had never heard in chapel before, and he knew that his moment had passed. When the youths started climbing out of the window he tried a little cackle, just to send them on their way.

'Oh, shut it,' said one of the boys.

'Shut it yourself,' said the girl who was climbing out behind him. 'It wasn't me.'

'Yeah, right,' came the reply, and they chattered

and tittered off into the night.

The Shortener had been badly shaken by his experience and immediately signed up for Mountwood, but he simply couldn't rid himself of the feeling that he was useless, washed-up, and would never be a ghost for the modern age.

At that moment there was a quiet tapping on the wall of his little room, and one of the sprites floated through. It was almost light and she was barely visible, but sprites are not really ghosts, and dawn and dusk present no serious problems for them.

'Hello there. Are you still up?'

'Er, yes, I am. Do come in'

'I was just wondering if you would do me a favour and partner me tomorrow in Miss Goneril's class. I want to do my best, you know, after what happened.' She shuddered slightly as she recalled her interview with Fredegonda.

'And you are such a fantastic materializer,' she added. 'So solid, I mean; you're almost real sometimes.'

'Oh well, thank you. But it's a gift, you know. No credit to me, I'm afraid.'

'That's silly; of course it's a credit to you. Will you help me?'

'What about the Phantom Welder? You seem to be great pals. Wouldn't he be a better choice?'

'I knew you would say that. But it's not like you think. He feels that he doesn't fit in, and tries to cover it up with his silly jokes. But I must do some serious work tomorrow; I'm not just an empty-headed blonde, even though I am empty.'

She was a forest spirit of Scandinavian descent,

and when she turned her back you could see that she was completely hollow.

The Shortener regretted his snide remark about the Welder at once. 'I'll be happy to help, if you think I can be of use.'

'Oh yes, of course you can. You are so . . . steady. Thank you. Until tomorrow night, then. We can meet up a bit earlier and rehearse.' And the sprite vanished.

The Shortener felt much better. By the time the first rays of the sun escaped the fir-clad ridge and leaped into the valley, he was at peace.

Twelve
Saving Markham Street

Charlotte and Daniel walked up through the iron posts to the park and sat down under General Markham. Every house on Markham Street had received the same official letter. As usual there was a bit of a wind blowing, not your typical cold dry easterly that keeps the beautiful beaches of the north-east swept clean of people even at the height of summer, but a mild gusty breeze from the south-west.

'Guess what,' said Charlotte, looking out over the city to the river in the distance. 'I've just realized for the first time why cranes are called cranes.'

'Oh?'

'Because they look like cranes.'

And Daniel saw that of course she was right. The huge skeletal cranes lining the river on the other side of town looked like great wading birds with big beaks about to pounce on some unsuspecting frog or minnow.

They were quiet for a long time. Then Charlotte said, 'We can stop this, Daniel. You can appeal to an independent inspector – I looked it up last night. If we oppose it, then they have to have an inquiry. We must protest, start a campaign. Save Markham Street.'

'It won't work,' said Daniel. 'My dad says that there is going to be a shopping centre as well, and that means not only the council against us but also all the big businesses who want to sell stuff. They have billions of pounds, and hundreds of clever lawyers.'

'But you always read in the papers about the little people fighting Big Business.'

'Yes, but not about them winning.'

Charlotte got horribly angry, suddenly, and to her annoyance even started to cry. 'So we just give up and go away, do we? You don't care enough, do you? Being sorry for yourself isn't the same thing as caring, you know. Caring is putting up a fight. Or maybe you don't have to bother, maybe you've got it all planned already, a nice place to move to, some new friends. And Mrs Wilder and Mr Jaros and Mrs Hughes's peonies can just lump it. Have you ever heard of Rosa Parks?'

Daniel shook his head.

'Well, there's a surprise.' And Charlotte walked off. But before she was out of earshot she stopped and turned round, and as a sudden gust whipped her hair around her tear-streaked face she shouted, 'Use your head, Daniel. What else is there to do?'

Daniel sat in misery for a while on General Markham's pedestal. Charlotte was wrong about one thing. They didn't have a nice place to move to.

As he wandered slowly home Daniel thought about the conversation over breakfast that morning. His father had tried to be cheerful, but Daniel knew him well enough. The great big house they lived in had been bought years ago, when nobody wanted to live in that kind of place. Now it was worth much more money, but it was in an awful state, particularly the bathroom, and they had borrowed a lot of money from the bank that would have to be paid back. They would never find anywhere like it.

When he got home his mother and father were in the living room, having one of those conversations that stop when someone comes in.

'Hello, Daniel, we were wondering where you had got to. Could you tell Aunt Joyce that supper is on the table?'

'No.'

'Daniel, for heaven's sake, this isn't easy for any of us, you know.'

Daniel said nothing, but turned and left the room, ran upstairs and threw himself down on his bed. They would have to move to some horrid place miles out of town, on a busy road, two bedrooms and a kitchen and a little living room where you couldn't even talk to each other because of the noise of the traffic outside. He knew very well that he was acting spoiled. He knew that lots of people lived very happy lives in small houses that they thought themselves lucky to have. But they didn't have Aunt Joyce. There would be a 'granny flat' built on top of the garage, and there she would be, forever – a plague, a pestilence, the Black Death – making all their lives a complete misery. And there would be no Charlotte to escape to, no General Markham, no Mr Jaros, no Swedish cinnamon buns, no Tompkins and no Jessie.

The next day the local paper carried a big headline on the front page: 'JOBS FOR THE REGION.'

Charlotte sat at the kitchen table and read it aloud to her mother, who was making breakfast and dressing Jonathan and George and wiping the baby's nose all at the same time.

'The local chamber of commerce predicts that the new Markham Park Retail Centre will create at least five hundred new jobs,' it began.

Then there was an interview with Jack Bluffit, Head of Planning, who talked a lot about regeneration, and getting things done, and bringing business to the city. The retail centre would have eco-friendly panels on the roof and there would be upmarket outlets. A chef who was famous from the television for using rude words and bullying people would open a restaurant.

'What's an upmarket outlet?' asked Jonathan.

'A place where a handbag costs more than a nurse earns in a year,' said Charlotte.

'Is it made of gold and diamonds?'

'No, it's made out of the skins of endangered animals, by children your age who get paid nothing at all,' said Charlotte crossly.

She was very unhappy. She knew that Daniel was as miserable as she was about having to move, and she wished she hadn't lost her rag yesterday. He was probably right. Nothing ever seemed to stop the demolishing and polluting and destruction of the city, or of the planet, if it came to that. She went up to her room and shut the door behind her. She was reading a book called *Slavery and Child Labour in Global Society* and it was doing nothing at all to cheer her up.

Daniel hadn't even got up that morning. It was a Saturday, so no school, and there didn't seem to be any point in getting out of bed. But as he lay there looking out of his window he felt something happening inside him.

He had woken with a sick feeling of despair, but

it seemed to be fading away and being replaced by something else. Anger. Not just anger. Rage.

'What else is there to do?' That was what Charlotte had shouted at him.

He thought about the doctors and nurses who operated in tents, trying to save the lives of children whose arms and legs had been blown off by bombs. They knew that there would be more bleeding children tomorrow, and the day after that. But what else was there to do? Then he remembered a girl he had read about who had been shot in the head just because she tried to go to school. It was in a country where some people thought girls shouldn't learn anything except how to cook and look after babies. She survived, and went on fighting for the rights of girls to go to school. What else was there to do?

Charlotte was wrong to think they had a chance. He was sure about that. But she was absolutely right that if you had to choose between fighting or lying down to be trampled on – well, it was a no-brainer.

Daniel got dressed and ran down the stairs. In the hall he bumped into Great-Aunt Joyce, who was coming out of the kitchen.

'Really, Daniel, you are so thoughtless. I must say . . .' Her voice trailed off. She had seen a look on his face that she had never seen before.

Daniel ran out of the house and across to number nine. He rang the bell. George opened the door.

'Hello, George. Is Charlotte in?'

'She's in her room. But I'm not allowed in. She's grumpy.'

'I'll risk it.'

Charlotte's door was firmly shut.

'Charlie, it's me. We have to talk.'

In her room Charlotte looked up from her book with a nice feeling in her stomach. If Daniel called her Charlie that was a good sign. A very good sign.

'Come in.'

Daniel started in as soon as he was in the room.

'I've been thinking. About Hector.'

'Hector?'

'Well, not only Hector, but he came into my mind when I was coming over here. Do you remember when we were doing the Greeks and the Trojans and Helen of Troy? Well, Hector is going out to fight Achilles, and his wife weeps and cries and says that he will surely die, and Hector knows that he will die and he points at his little son and says, "When he walks down the street, people will say, *There goes the son of Hector the warrior*." That's what mattered to him. Not winning. Winning doesn't matter.'

Charlotte smiled. She looked at him standing there solidly, with his mop of uncombed hair and his hazel eyes glaring at her. She should have known better. Daniel was a slow starter. He needed time to think. But once he had decided, he was like a badger. He bit hard, and he didn't let go until he heard bones crack.

'All right. If you are going to be Hector, who shall I be?'

They thought about that for a while. Charlotte considered Joan of Arc, but she was burned at the stake, and that was just too much. They decided on Boudicca, queen of the Iceni, who faced down the might of the Roman legions, and lost.

When that was settled, Charlotte said, 'The first thing is to talk to everyone on the street. We have to make sure there are objections, and as many people as possible must register a protest.'

Thirteen
Lord Ridget

Jack Bluffit was in a frightful temper. His temper was partly caused by the ache in his backside. Every time he sat down he yelped and had to stand up again. And to make matters worse, there was going to be an inquiry. He took some deep breaths. Just more work to do.

'Snyder!'

Frederick oiled his way into the office. 'Did you call, Mr Bluffit?'

He knew very well that Jack had called. Everyone on the top floor had heard him.

'There shouldn't be any serious problems with this blasted inquiry. As far as I can see, there's only a bunch of old biddies and arty-farty types and benefit scroungers to deal with.'

'Well, sir,' said Frederick, 'perhaps to be on the safe side . . . to avoid unnecessary risks . . . it might be possible . . .'

'What? Spit it out, Snyder.'

'Some information about the condition of the street might be of use.'

'Right, I get it. Get me Health and Safety, Fire Department, Department of Works, the lot. I want to see them today.'

'They are on their way, sir.'

'Are they?' Bluffit stared at Fredrick. Sometimes he

thought the man was so sharp he might cut himself.

Snyder slithered out.

The most important thing was to get the right person to hold the inquiry. Someone who wouldn't let him down. Jack knew just the man. He reached for the telephone and dialled.

The voice at the other end was very well-bred.

'Lord Ridget speaking.'

'It's Bluffit.'

'Yes, oh, hello, how are you feeling? Shame about that little tumble the other weekend. The old mare's usually very docile. Bit hard in the mouth perhaps. And of course, not used to being kicked and hit. We don't usually go for that kind of thing.'

'That nag would be at the knacker's yard by now if I had my way.'

'Oh, I'm sure you don't mean that. Long and faithful service, you know. Out to pasture . . .'

'Out to pasture my foot. I don't have time for all this nonsense, Ridget. I know why you invited me to your place. It wasn't for my pretty face. You thought you could soft-soap me into stopping the plans for building on your land. Well, I can tell you that the affordable-housing scheme is going ahead anyway. Lots of poor people, you know, and some asylum seekers – they have to live somewhere.'

'Oh dear, oh dear. You cannot imagine how terrible it is for us. All that hard work reconstituting the bed, and planting the banks, and I had four rods on it last year, and probably six this year. They said I couldn't do it, but I jolly well showed 'em, I said they'd come back, and they did.'

'Who came back?'

'The salmon, of course. After forty years. Your beastly scheme will spoil everything. Houses right on the riverbank. There might be litter louts or even – what d'you call 'ems? – chivs.'

'Chavs.'

'That's it. Is it really not possible to build somewhere else? It is such a lovely spot. The Laird of Rothmull came down last year, and even he was impressed. He showed me his flies.'

'He what?'

'He had a lovely Black-Green Highlander that he swore by.'

'I bet he did. Look, Ridget, stop talking gobbledegook and listen. There is a small chance you might be off the hook. I shouldn't be telling you this, but . . .'

'What? What shouldn't you be telling me?'

'Can you keep your mouth shut?'

'Of course, my dear man. Mum's the word. Soul of discretion, lips sealed and all that.'

'Well, it looks as if the council might have overstretched themselves a bit. Money's short. There's a big redevelopment planned, dead pricey, and it's just been approved. If they actually build it, they'll have to abandon your scheme. Of course, with a great big redevelopment like that, there are objections. There's going to be an inquiry; who knows what will happen?'

'Goodness gracious! I shall have to cross my fingers like mad.'

'You might be able to do more than that,' said Jack.

They talked for a few more minutes. Then Jack hung up.

'Daft old git,' he muttered.

Daniel and Charlotte had worked very hard. They had visited every house on the street, making sure that as many people as possible wrote in good time to dispute the Compulsory Purchase Order, so there had to be an inquiry. But getting an inquiry is just the beginning. You have to win your case. It's not enough to say that you like your house and don't want to move. You have to be able to prove that the new motorway will be a terrible disturbance and destroy the environment, or that the new shopping centre will be built right on top of the place where the only pair of web-footed hoopy-birds left in the British Isles make their nest. Or else you have to show that the street is of great historical importance, with a Roman fort or a famous battlefield just under the pavement; or that the houses are very important examples of nineteenth-century urban development, designed by a very important architect.

None of this was particularly easy, because Markham Street, although the houses were pretty old, was just a street, and the park was just a park. Nobody had ever heard of there being anything in particular under it, and in the park there were mostly just pigeons and starlings, and the town was already so noisy and full of cars that some more noise was hardly going to make much difference. But people did their best.

Mrs Wilder, who was writing another detective story, put her work aside and spent days looking through old historical documents about the city, to try to find something important that had happened just on the site of Markham Street. Even Daniel's new neighbours, the Bosse-Lynches, although they were just as stuck-up and snooty as Daniel had expected, did their bit.

Mr Bosse-Lynch wrote long letters to the newspapers, complaining about commercial interests lowering the value of a residential area, and the rise in crime, and the country generally going to the dogs, and the pitifully small compensation he had been offered. Daylight robbery, he called it. Free Englishmen were being mugged by the council, he wrote. He also wrote that the chairman of the council was a crypto-Stalinist, but that bit didn't get printed, because the newspaper was afraid they would be sued for libel.

One person who gave them some real hope was Jim Dawson, who lived with his partner Peter Richards at number three. He worked in the zoology department at the university.

'Birds are all very well,' he said to Charlotte and Daniel one day, when they met on the street, 'but there's not much chance of finding anything of note in the park. Something small, that's your best bet. Doesn't even have to be an insect or a worm. Lichens, mosses, moulds. Nobody has much idea about what has evolved in these old half-polluted city biotopes. Something genuinely unique of that kind might make them think twice.'

So now the children of Markham Street and the streets nearby had something useful to do after school. They all crawled all over the park with tins and jam jars, collecting bugs and beetles and worms and woodlice and spiders. They scraped moss and mildew from stones and green algae from benches and from the bark of expiring trees.

Charlotte's small brothers were in seventh heaven. Every day, covered in dirt from the day's exertions, they waited outside number three for Jim to come home, so that they could show him the day's harvest, and he always looked carefully and said, 'Mmm, that's interesting,' or, 'Oh, what have we here?' But he never got really excited.

In spite of all their efforts, the Markham Street residents weren't getting very far. And there was something else. One day when Daniel came home from school there was a van parked outside the house. On the side were the words 'County Surveyor'. In the hall Great-Aunt Joyce was talking to a young man in a suit. He had lots of pens in his top pocket and a clipboard, and a piece of apparatus in his other hand that looked like some kind of meter.

'Oh yes,' Great-Aunt Joyce was saying in her moany voice, 'terrible, really not hygienic at all. It should certainly be looked at. I shouldn't be surprised if there are nasty bacteria. One can catch things; I have a very sensitive immune system. That boy, I don't think he washes his hands properly after, you know . . .'

'What boy?' asked Daniel, dropping his bag on the hall floor.

'Oh, Daniel, I didn't see you. You must not creep up on people like that. This gentleman is from the surveyor's office. They are surveying the street.'

'Yes, hello,' said the man, 'but we are only doing a structural survey. Foundations, walls, that kind of thing. As I said, the state of the bathroom isn't our business.' He was embarrassed. 'Anyway, I'm all done here, so I'll be off next door.'

'Bring a cup of tea to my room, Daniel,' said Great-Aunt Joyce, turning to go upstairs. 'I don't know where your mother has got to. She really shouldn't expect me to answer the door. She is fully aware of my legs.'

Mr Jaros got a visit too. Not from the surveyors but from the health-and-safety inspectors. After they had gone he sat by the stove and worried.

The two ladies who had come to visit him had seemed very friendly, and he had offered them a biscuit and a cup of coffee. But they had left a list that was two pages long of things that were wrong with his workshop. Fire hazard, commercial premises, emergency exit, risk assessment, extractor fan . . . The words jumbled and jostled in his head. It just went on and on. He liked the smell of glue and resin and turpentine, and those fans sounded like jet engines. How could he listen to Smetana and Dvořák with a fan roaring away? But the worst bit came at the end of the list. Something about domestic animals in high-risk industrial environments. He guessed that the domestic animal must be Jessie, and the high-risk industrial environment must be his workbench. But she had lain beside it for almost thirteen years.

'Ah, Jess,' he said, and she opened one eye and thumped her tail, 'What is all this about?' Jessie didn't know. Or if she did, she wasn't saying.

'The inquiry is to be led by Lord Ridget,' said Jim Dawson that evening, as he and Peter were making supper in their kitchen.

'That old goat? I thought he just hunted and

fished and wrote letters to the newspapers about people going for walks across his grouse moors and disturbing the birds he's going to kill.'

'He does now, but he used to be a judge before he retired. He was in the news once; he was trying a man for mugging someone and stealing his trainers. Ridget said, "What on earth are trainers?" And the barrister replied, "I think you might know them as plimsolls, m'lud." They called him Rip van Ridget.'

'Why dig him up suddenly? There must be a reason.'

'There is. I rang Sam Norton on the local paper this morning. He always knows what's going on behind the scenes.'

'And?'

'He said he smelled a rat. He said that Ridget is in Jack Bluffit's pocket; he'll do anything he wants. Bluffit knows what he's doing. He's counting on Ridget to make sure the inquiry goes his way.'

'So what are our chances, Jim?'

'Very thin indeed, I'd say.'

Fourteen
The Dark of the Moon

Fredegonda was rounding off the evening's lecture, the fourth in her series 'Spectral Theory and Human Psychology'.

'So, to summarize our conclusions,' she said, 'first – the vast majority of humans are surprisingly squeamish about suppurating excrescences, that is to say pustules, abscesses, ulcers, blisters, pimples, spots, carbuncles and the like. Also, putrefying or maggoty flesh, especially when still connected to a living body, usually arouses a satisfyingly negative response. Secondly, do not forget our little motto: "More is better." A single infected abscess on the nose or cheek might even arouse sympathy, and we don't want that, do we? But a face and body entirely covered with an infestation of pussy boils can hardly fail to have the desired effect. Finally, I would like to leave you with a little tip – hospital waste. Tissues, organs, amputated body parts, blood and bodily fluids can be great sources of inspiration.'

She glanced out of the window set high in the wall, where a few stars glittered.

'Time for a break. Please be here again in an hour for your practical work with Miss Goneril.'

When she had left the hall the ghosts relaxed and chatted to each other for a while.

The Phantom Welder said, 'I didn't get much of

that. What's an excrescence when it's at home?'

'Why don't you ask the Druid?' said Iphigenia. 'He knows any amount of words.'

She knew that the Druid was still smarting from his experience the other night and had been avoiding the Welder. So the Welder glided over to the Druid, who went a bit transparent when he approached, and would have gone pale if he could have been any paler.

'I need some help here, mate,' said the Welder.' I'm all over the place.'

'I don't think so,' said the Druid. 'All your parts appear to be connected at the moment.'

'I mean I don't get what that Miss Fredegonda's on about. Look,' he went on, for he knew very well why the Druid was avoiding him, 'I didn't mean anything by it. It's just me and my big mouth.'

'Well,' said the Druid, 'how can I help?'

The ice was broken, and the Druid took the Welder aside and explained at length about suppuration and infestation and other long words that Fredegonda had used.

Meanwhile Ron Peabody had drifted outside to do some deep breathing and a few stomach curls. He wanted to shine in the practical class – it was his strong suit, after all. His wife always smiled gently and told him that true haunting was an art, not a science, and no doubt she was right about that. She was much cleverer than him. But there was something to be said for a really fit ghost of the old school. Just go straight at 'em and scare 'em stiff. No fancy stuff, that was the thing. Like Lord Nelson at Trafalgar.

Ron started thinking about his son, Percy. He

was a bit of a softy, it couldn't be denied, and Ron wished Iphigenia would see that. There was nothing wrong with poetry – he himself was fond of a bit of noble verse. But all these birds and butterflies were sapping the lad's willpower, and willpower was the most important thing of all. He should know. Once in his life he had lacked willpower, and look what had happened.

Ron stared gloomily into the darkness of the courtyard and his thoughts turned yet again to that fateful week in his life. Oh, how he had worked! Honing his body to perfection, swimming for hours up and down the Thames, with the tide, against the tide, across the tide. At last he had been ready to go where no man had gone before. Nobody had ever swum the English Channel. They said it was impossible, but he, Ron Peabody, was going to do it. And then, that evening, the visit to the theatre, and the glorious vision on stage. Love at first sight. Love? No, adulation, worship.

For three nights in a row he had simply gazed at the miracle that was Iphigenia, all else forgotten. And he had won her heart. A week later, that newspaper headline had screamed at him from every street corner, every paperboy yelling out the news: 'Captain Webb swims the English Channel.'

He had learned a grim lesson then. Willpower. He had found the love of his life but the price had been high indeed. If he had waited, controlled himself, he could have been famous forever. Instead he threw himself headlong into ecstasy, and missed the goal of his life. He had found some comfort in other goals; the Bristol Channel had never been swum, nor the

Irish sea. But still . . . willpower, that was the thing.

Ron pulled himself together, dismissing the past from his mind. It was time to return to class.

'Now then,' said Goneril, when the ghosts had drifted in after their break, 'I want you all completely visible and attentive. Make a ring, please. Kylie, perhaps you should show us what you can do.'

Kylie wasn't the tree-sprite's real name, or rather, she didn't actually have a name, but the Welder had said she looked a bit like some pop star he had seen a picture of, and the name had stuck.

'I've asked the Shortener to help me,' she announced, as she floated into the centre of the ring of spectres. 'He is going to play the human.'

The Shortener stood up shyly, and taking off his bowler hat he made a little bow. Then he concentrated very hard, and gradually the faint wavery luminescence that is normal for a ghost faded, and he became so firm that no one who met him on the street would ever suspect that he was an apparition and not solid flesh.

A wave of ghostly applause fluttered around the ring. And now the young sprite advanced towards him. She really was charming – beautiful big eyes, blonde hair that hung like a soft curtain around a heart-shaped face, a wide smiling mouth and even a little dimple in her left cheek.

With an enchanting smile she held out her hands towards the Shortener, and in a low breathy voice she murmured, 'Oh, you handsome stranger – please come to my arms. I need to be held. I long to be embraced.'

The Phantom Welder muttered, 'Blimey,' but luckily for him he was on the other side of the ring from Goneril, who was completely focused on Kylie, studying her every move.

Then the sprite stopped, as though overtaken by shyness, and lowered her head. Her hair tumbled forward like a golden veil, covering her features. The Shortener had rather lost his concentration. He was a very fine materializer but a very poor actor, and he just stood there.

'Now!' hissed the sprite, from underneath her hair.

'Ooh, er, sorry,' said the Shortener.

Then he lifted his arms, spread them wide and advanced towards the Sprite. Everyone could see that he was a bit embarrassed, but they willed him to go on. He approached the magical figure before him, and when his arms were almost embracing her, she lifted her head and the curtain of hair fell back as she raised her face to his. It was covered in huge boils, some of which had burst, her nose was half eaten away by some rotting disease, her open lips were dry and cracked and between them her tongue could be seen, infested with yellowy green pustules.

'Give us a kiss, then, sweetheart,' she croaked.

'Oh, oh, oh,' said the Shortener, as he had been told to. He wasn't really horrified, that goes without saying, and he wasn't any good at pretending to be horrified either, but he did his best, and the sprite's performance was impressive.

A spontaneous round of applause broke out among the ghostly group, with a 'Jolly well done!' from Ron Peabody.

The sprite's boils disappeared in an instant, and

with a satisfied smile she bobbed a little curtsy and joined the others.

'Well, I must say,' said Goneril, 'you have obviously been putting your back into it . . . if you see what I mean,' she added, remembering that the sprite didn't have a back. 'That was an excellent piece of work.'

Fifteen
Mrs Wilder Speaks Out

The Public Inquiry into the Compulsory Purchase Orders for the Redevelopment of Markham Park and Environs was held in one of the county courtrooms close by City Hall. The room was fairly full. Some of the audience were just there out of curiosity, and there was a whole Year Eight class who were there as part of their Citizenship Studies course. Most of the residents of Markham Street had showed up, and a couple of reporters, and the front row was occupied by a lot of men in suits. In the middle of the row sat a man with his arms crossed and his stubby legs planted firmly on the floor. Daniel could only see the back of his head, his thick neck in a tight collar and his heavy shoulders.

'That's Jack Bluffit,' said Peter Richards, when he saw where Daniel was looking.

Next to Jack sat Frederick Snyder, with a briefcase beside his chair. His eyes slid about the room, taking in the audience, and he looked very pleased with himself.

Lord Ridget entered, tall and thin and elegantly dressed in a well-tailored suit, and took his place at the front of the room facing the public. After him came the county clerk with a folder under his arm; he sat down in a chair slightly behind and to the side. Lord Ridget was wearing a pair of half-moon spectacles that his wife had told him made him look more intelligent. They didn't help much. He had vague blue eyes that seemed about to pop out of his head, a long nose and almost no chin. None of this was his fault; these things happen in families where people marry their own relations over hundreds of years. He might have been a warm and thoughtful person in spite of it, but he wasn't.

He opened the inquiry by flapping his hand at the clerk, who stood up and read aloud for a very long time about the proposed motorway and shopping centre. Then, one after another, the suited men in the front row stood up and spoke about how important it was to make way for modernization, regeneration, urbanization and a lot of other –ations.

The residents of Markham Street were sitting together in a row near the back. Daniel and Charlotte were next to Mrs Wilder. She had her best black coat on, and a pair of fur-lined boots. Her grey hair had been nicely done in a bun by Mrs Hughes. She looked very proper, not at all wispy and dressed-in-a-hurry as she sometimes did at home. She leaned forward with one hand on the handle of her stick and the other cupped behind her ear so as to catch what was said.

For a while Lord Ridget tried to look as though he was listening intelligently to everything, but fairly soon he gave up; there is only so much you can do with a brain that gets very little exercise. Soon he leaned back in his chair, looking sheepish, and closed his eyes. He tried wrinkling his forehead, so that the audience would suppose he was thinking, but nobody was taken in. He was bored to death and half asleep already. When at last the suits had finished,

114

the clerk leaned forward and coughed in his ear.

'Eh? Oh yes.' Lord Ridget sat up. 'The objections will now be heard.' He slumped back into his chair.

Peter Richards stood up and made his way to the front. He was a fine violinist, and could have played in any orchestra in the country. But he had chosen to work in the city where he had been born and brought up. Now he made a moving speech about the beautiful old cityscape, its churches and chapels, its docklands, its terraced houses sweeping down to the river, so much a part of the northern industrial heritage.

'This heritage must be preserved at all costs,' he finished.

The Markham residents clapped.

As soon as he was done, the chunky figure of Jack Bluffit rose from the front row.

'Now, my lord, I will make my report,' he said, in his harsh no-nonsense voice. 'This so-called heritage is on its last legs. The place is falling down and ripe for demolition. I have the surveyor's report here.'

Frederick Snyder had opened his briefcase. He handed Jack a folder already open at the right page. Jack looked down at it.

'There is subsidence, the buildings' foundations are unstable, the sewage system is a hundred and fifty years old, the road surface is shot to pieces and needs major maintenance,' he said, stabbing his stubby finger at the paper as he spoke. 'We have estimated the cost of bringing Markham Street up to a reasonable standard, and it runs to millions. A lot of millions,' he added for good measure.

Daniel and Charlotte looked at each other. Now

they understood what that man with the pens in his pocket had been doing.

Jack Bluffit wasn't finished. 'And that's not all,' he said, his voice rising in indignation. 'I have discovered that in Markham Street some very shady business goes on, conducted in a private residence: unsanitary, unsafe, child labour being used. It should be stopped.' Bluffit looked around feeling pleased with himself. With a bit of luck those reporters would pick up on the child-labour bit; that was always newsworthy.

Mr Jaros, sitting next to Mrs Wilder and trying to follow the proceedings, thought, Who could that be? I'm the only person with a business on Markham Street.

Then it struck him. In a rage he leaped out of his seat and started gesticulating and shouting things in Czech. This was actually a good thing, because if he had told Jack Bluffit in English what he was going to do to him (it included rope and rusty pitchforks) he would have been arrested.

Lord Ridget looked very startled. Then he grabbed his gavel and started banging it madly on the bench in front of him. 'Stop it, silence, be quiet! This is not a public house.'

But Mr Jaros seemed unable to stop, until Mrs Wilder tugged at his sleeve and said gently, 'Please, Fjodor, sit down.'

With a great effort Mr Jaros got a hold on himself and dropped back into his chair, sinking into a miserable silence with his head in his hands.

'That didn't do us much good,' whispered Daniel.

'You can say that again,' Charlotte replied.

Now Jim Dawson stood up and moved to the

front of the room. Daniel and Charlotte crossed their fingers. In a quiet voice he spoke of a centipede that little George had found under a waste bin in the park. It showed some interesting anomalies in the second and thirteenth segments.

Lord Ridget appeared to be in a coma.

Jack Bluffit turned in his chair and started signalling to someone sitting in the row behind him. A kind-looking gentleman with a moustache and a red waistcoat stood up.

'Hello, Jim,' he said.

'Hello, Professor Manley,' Jim replied.

'I am not here entirely voluntarily,' said the professor, 'but as you know I am among other things Scientific Advisor to the Department of the Environment, and I must fulfil the duties that this entails.'

'Of course, sir,' said Jim. He liked and admired Professor Manley. Loved him really. They had spent many happy days on the moors together with their butterfly nets and collecting tins back when Jim had been a student.

'Well then, I am aware that you are a resident of Markham Street, but now I speak to you as a fellow naturalist. Can you truthfully say, Jim, as a scientist and a man of honour, that the morphology of this centipede is of unique scientific interest?'

Their eyes met. There was a silence that seemed to go on for a long time, though it was probably only a few seconds.

'No,' said Jim.

The professor smiled in sad sympathy. Jim went back to his seat. Peter put an arm round his shoulders.

Daniel looked at Charlotte again. 'From bad to worse,' he said.

Now Bluffit was leaning forward in his seat, grimacing at Lord Ridget and making a chopping movement with his hand.

Lord Ridget peered at him. 'What? Oh.' He cleared his throat. 'That seems to bring things to a conclusion.'

'Not quite.' A calm and very distinct voice spoke out. It came from Mrs Wilder, who now got to her feet, leaning on her stick. 'I have something to add.'

Lord Ridget looked at Jack Bluffit, who had sunk back in his chair again. Bluffit shrugged his shoulders, as though to say, 'What do I care? That old baggage can hardly make a difference.'

Daniel was thinking, 'Oh no, please, don't let her be made to look a fool.'

'In Markham Park,' Mrs Wilder began, 'right in the middle, is a statue of General Sir George Markham, who as I am sure we are all aware fought and died for his country in a foreign land. However, perhaps not everyone knows that the park, and the statue, and the streets around the park, are built on what was once Markham land. For General Markham was not only a soldier. He cared about the people of this city, and he bequeathed the land to them, to be enjoyed as a place of rest and recreation in perpetuity. Well, maybe I'm getting old, but I thought that "in perpetuity" meant "forever". But apparently it means something else. It means "until Jack Bluffit wants something".'

At this the reporters, who had been looking very bored, sat up, grinned at each other and started scribbling in their notebooks.

'Let's see how Bluffit takes that,' whispered one of them to his neighbour.

Jack didn't take it very well. His face turned a very dangerous-looking purplish red colour, as though he had swallowed a large dumpling that had only got halfway to his stomach before wedging itself tight.

Mrs Wilder was just warming up. 'Being interested in the arts,' she said, 'I am acquainted with a number of painters and sculptors, and I am assured on very good authority that a certain Mr Snyder has been making enquiries about the creation of a large equestrian statue, to stand at the centre of the new retail park. Mr Snyder is Jack Bluffit's personal assistant, and need I add that the statue will not be a statue of Jack Bluffit's personal assistant.'

At this Snyder's head swivelled round on his thin neck and he stared intently at Mrs Wilder. His face was expressionless. Jack Bluffit's neck was now puce with touches of crimson.

'Is it possible,' she said, 'is it even thinkable, that the wanton destruction of a whole city neighbourhood has been set in train to satisfy one man's personal vanity? I do not wish to accuse, of course. I merely ask.'

Jack Bluffit exploded out of his chair and roared, 'That is slander, Lord Ridget. That is defamation of a faithful servant of this city. Strike it from the record. I'll sue if this goes on.'

'Er, I think that's enough now,' said Ridget to Mrs Wilder. He looked worriedly at Jack's swollen features and tight collar, wondering if the council would build on his riverbank if Bluffit had a heart attack.

'But I haven't quite finished, my lord,' said Mrs Wilder politely. 'If I may just add some concluding remarks – on another topic,' she added.

'Oh, very well then. But keep off the personal stuff.'

'Of course, my lord.' She went on. 'The Markham family have always been soldiers. General Markham's son fought at Ypres, and his grandson was tragically killed during the defence of Tobruk in 1941, while hunting the Desert Fox.'

This impressed everybody in the room except Jack Bluffit; General Rommel, nicknamed the Desert Fox, was the most brilliant and wily commander of the German forces in the Second World War. Henry Markham must have been quite a man. Mrs Wilder was not being untruthful, she would never be that, but she had chosen her words carefully. Henry Markham *had* died in North Africa, and he *was* hunting the desert fox at the time, but it was a real desert fox that had been nosing around the dustbins outside the mess tent. Henry came from a good family and had had an expensive education, so he couldn't resist slaughtering innocent animals; catching sight of the creature, he had grabbed a sub-machine gun, shouted, 'Halloo!' and 'Tally-ho!' and rushed out into the night, stepping on one of the land mines at the camp perimeter that he himself had laid only a few hours earlier.

'I have been in communication with Henry Markham's son William, now living in Marbella,' continued Mrs Wilder, 'and I would like to conclude by reading out his letter to me.' She read:

Dear Mrs Wilder,

It comes as shock to me to hear that Markham Park is to be desecrated. I know that it meant a great deal to my great-grandfather, and he certainly intended it to remain untouched as a gift to the people of the city. It is such a lovely spot, is it not? What a shame that tradition and heritage should be brushed aside for commercial gain and so-called modernization. Is there really nothing to be done? Surely someone will step into the breach and save the park and its neighbourhood?

Yours sincerely,
William Markham, Bart.

There was a PS that said that if they took away the statue and sold it, then Mrs Wilder should send the money to him in Marbella, but she didn't read out that bit.

Mrs Wilder sat down. With both hands on her stick, she stared fixedly at Lord Ridget, as though expecting something to happen. Daniel heard her mutter something that sounded like, 'Come on, you imbecile, think.'

Lord Ridget was sitting up, and a pained expression came over his face as he tried to get his brain to work. Finally he spoke. 'Er, who was that letter from, did you say?'

'William Markham, my lord.'

'Markham? One of the Markhams of Futtering Burnside?'

'That's correct. The family seat is at Burnside, and their land marches with yours, I believe.'

'Yes, yes, of course it does. But ... that must be Lugsy Markham. Good grief! He fagged for me at school. Huge ears, stuck out like soup plates ... Well, well, dear me, that's a different kettle of fish. Tradition ... Heritage ... Oh dear ...'

And the inquiry was over.

Sixteen
Pathetic Percy

In the early morning after Kylie's boils exercise, Ron and Iphigenia had a row. They were on the whole a very happy couple, perhaps because they were so different, but even the happiest couples sometimes get themselves into a tangle.

As they were preparing to snuggle down and disappear for the day, Ron said casually, 'Fine head of hair on that sprite, I must say.'

Iphigenia was silent for a while. She might not have been a young enchantress with a dimple in her cheek, but at least she wasn't completely empty; and as far as hair was concerned, well, a very famous painter called Mr Rossetti had seen her perform at the theatre once, and afterwards he had come round to her dressing room and said that he wanted to paint her wonderful copper-coloured hair. She had almost agreed, until she realized that he wanted to paint the rest of her too, in a bath with no clothes on.

'I have heard that gentlemen prefer blondes, Ronald,' said Iphigenia. This told Ron all he needed to know – he had put his foot in it, and then some. She had called him Ronald, and her voice reminded him of the mummified pharaoh whom they had chatted with once on a trip to the British Museum.

'Oh no, m'dear, that's absurd, I didn't mean . . . I was only . . .'

But of course it was too late.

'You don't have to defend yourself, Ronald. You have a perfect right to express an opinion.'

Then Ron, as husbands always do, began to feel hurt and misunderstood.

'Now, Iffy, you know very well what I meant. Nothing at all.'

'Nothing? I saw you staring at her. I suppose you thought she gave a wonderful performance.'

'Well, I wouldn't say that. But it was pretty good, er, wasn't it . . . ?' he finished lamely.

'It was childish and the work of a rank amateur. We aren't supposed to be playing charades here.'

'But . . .'

Iphigenia turned away. 'Percy, my darling,' she called, 'Come here, sweetest. There is a lovely sonnet about daffodils that I want you to hear before bed.'

But now Ron, glaring at Iphigenia from his skinless face, shouted, 'Percy, me lad, let's try that handspring again; you nearly got it last time.'

Percy appeared between his two parents. He looked up at his mother, then at his father.

'Oh, oh, oh!' he said, and faded from view.

Percy had been having rather a boring time at Mountwood. He sat in on most of the classes, but nobody paid him much attention, and everybody thought he was too young to do any serious haunting. Young ghosts – murdered children and suchlike – can be very frightening if the atmosphere is right, but there is not much one can do to develop skills. They are just dead children. But then Percy had found Samson, and that cheered him up a bit.

Samson had been abandoned by his mother, and when Percy first met him he was standing uncertainly in front of a cornered rat in the byre. His back was arched, his tortoiseshell tail was stiff as a bottle-brush, but although he was very hungry he couldn't quite summon up the courage for the final spring. The rat was bigger than he was, and was standing up baring its yellow teeth at him and chattering unpleasantly. When Percy appeared, the rat saw its chance and scuttled off. After that Percy and Samson got to know each other. It was nice having a cat because, cats being what they are, it didn't matter whether Percy was visible or not, and that was peaceful. Cats have a sixth sense as well as nine lives.

So it was to the byre that Percy fled from his rowing parents.

'It's all my fault. I'm just Pathetic Percy,' he said to Samson, when he had found him curled up in the straw. 'I'll never make them pleased with me, I'll never have proper friends and I'll never be frightful.'

Percy knew that he would be a young child forever. He would never grow up. Ghosts don't do that; they are what they are. But couldn't he change inside himself? Become different? What kind of different though?

His father wanted him to be manly, and he did try to do press-ups, but it wasn't easy in a nightdress and although Ron didn't say that he was disappointed, and was always very cheerful, Percy could feel it.

His mother wanted him to love poetry and remember long and difficult things. At this very moment he should have been practising something that started 'Blow, blow, thou winter wind, thou art not so unkind . . .' He could do the beginning bit, and the end, which went '. . . As friend remembered not.' But the middle just would not stick in his mind.

Percy missed Daniel and Charlotte. They weren't remembered not, they were remembered. For more than a century he hadn't had any other children to talk to, dead or alive, so meeting the two of them had been very special. He almost wished he hadn't been so weak and sorry for himself when he missed the bus. If he hadn't made such a fuss, then they wouldn't have been in such a hurry to find Mountwood and take him home. Could he have been braver? He just didn't know, and Samson didn't care one way or the other, because he was a cat, and cats aren't in the least bit interested in becoming better or braver or cleverer. They are interested in mice and birds and keeping clean and watching out for dogs.

So as the sun climbed higher in the sky, and Iphigenia and Ronald vanished into separate corners of the mouldy boot room that they occupied in the castle, Percy curled up beside Samson in the straw of the byre and sadly dematerialized.

In the city the morning traffic clogged the main thoroughfares. The honking of horns and the wailing of a siren floated up to the top floor of the Department of Planning, where Jack Bluffit was waiting impatiently for his visitor. At last there was a timid tapping on the door and Snyder oozed into the room.

'Lord Ridget has arrived.'

'Well, get him in here.'

Snyder disappeared, to be replaced by the gangling figure of Lord Ridget. His eyes stuck out even more than usual and worried lines furrowed his brow.

'Right,' said Jack. 'Time's up. I need a result.'

'It's most frightfully difficult, I've been thinking about it all weekend, lost some sleep over it. Tossing and turning.'

'Poor you.'

'I really don't see how I can let this go through, you know. Lugsy's letter shook me up. I mean, he's right, isn't he? Everything is just getting bulldozed away, all the old houses and the way things used to be. There was a burn not far from Markham Park that I fished when I was a little chap. Just tiddlers, of course, roach mostly; you know, a float and a little bit of bacon rind, but they said there were bream, although I never saw one . . .'

'What's this got to do with anything?' growled Bluffit impatiently. Surely this dolt wasn't about to mess things up for him?

'Well, I mean, it's gone, vanished. You can't find the burn anywhere. It runs underneath the city bypass. It's part of the sewage system! Imagine the poor fish trying to swim in sewage!'

At that moment Jack Bluffit was imagining Lord Ridget swimming in sewage, but he gritted his teeth and said, 'Right then, if you are going to stop the Markham Park development, I'll just give the contractor a ring. He's waiting for the go-ahead from me to move in and start making a right old mess of your precious riverbank.' He reached out to the telephone and picked up the receiver.

'No, stop, hang on! Wait!' yelped Lord Ridget.

Bluffit put the receiver down again. 'Well?'

Lord Ridget collapsed into a chair like a puppet whose strings had been cut. His face was a picture of melancholy and despair. He put his head in his hands and groaned. In a few months he would look out of his bedroom window and see, not the ancient willows lining his peaceful river, but houses and motorbikes and people. In his mind's eye he saw them throwing plastic bottles and cigarette ends into the river, dumping rusty bicycles. There might even be children who paddled. It was no good; he simply could not bear it.

He sighed deeply, took a gold fountain pen from his inside pocket and signed the document that Jack Bluffit thrust under his well-bred nose.

When he had gone, shaking his head and mumbling to himself, Jack sat down at his desk. Things were working out. They always did.

He started happily looking over the plans for the new development. He would have to make sure that no buildings or traffic signs spoilt the view of the statue from the main road. A few years ago some idiots on a council had spent a huge amount of money on a great big sculpture and plonked it down on a hill a mile or two outside their city. It was supposed to be some kind of angel; it looked more like a rusty aeroplane to him. But it had to be admitted, after a year or two it had become a landmark for the whole area. Everybody knew about it; every tired motorist coming back from the south saw it and thought, There it is, I'm home. The trick was visibility. Lines of sight.

Jack was making a few notes in pencil on the blueprints when Snyder appeared in the room carrying a tray.

'What are you doing here? You're supposed to knock.'

128

'I did, Mr Bluffit.'

'Are you calling me a liar?'

'Absolutely not, Mr Bluffit. You, sir? Such a pillar of honesty, such an ornament to the city, a liar – never.'

Jack looked at him sharply. Was Snyder making fun of him? He'd better not be.

Frederick caught Jack's look, and his eyes darted about the room. He wondered if he had gone too far this time. His hands trembled, and the coffee cup on the tray jiggled and tinkled in its saucer.

'It's eleven o'clock, sir.'

Coffee time. Jack reached out for his cup.

'Where's the paper? What's got into you today?'

'Ah, the paper. I may have mislaid it, sir.'

'Mislaid it? You've never mislaid anything in your life. What's going on?'

Snyder didn't speak.

'Shove off and get it.'

Snyder left the room and returned quite soon with the morning paper, folded carefully, held out in front of him at arm's length. He dropped it on the desk, and before a surprised Jack Bluffit could say anything, he turned on his heel and almost ran out of the room.

Jack heard his rapid footsteps pattering away down the corridor. Then he took a sip of his coffee, leaned back in his chair and unfolded the paper. A huge banner headline covered almost the entire front page.

BLUFFIT BLUFFS IT

Underneath, in smaller print, it said 'Markham Street pensioner gives Bluffit a going-over. *See pages 2–4.*'

As he read the article, Jack's face darkened. His eyes narrowed, and the grinding of his teeth could be heard in the next room, where a secretary thought something had gone wrong with the copying machine and rang down to the service department to get it fixed. Sam Norton, the author of the article, had had great fun. He made a big thing of the frail old woman who had taken the lid off Bluffit's schemes (he called it 'opening a can of worms') and mocked Lord Ridget mercilessly, suggesting that Bluffit had hauled him in to lead the inquiry only because a sack of potatoes couldn't be dressed in a suit. He had ended the article with a question: 'How much longer can Jack Bluffit be allowed to treat our city as his personal property?'

With his meaty hands Jack scrunched the newspaper into a ball and hurled it across the room, missing the waste-paper basket by at least a yard. He got up from his desk and paced up and down for a while, imagining all the things he would do to Sam Norton if he ever met him in a dark alley. But after a while he calmed down a bit. Why should he care about being trashed by some little rat of a reporter. Norton was nobody, a cockroach. And nothing could stop him now. Ridget had done his bit. Markham Street was going into the dustbin of history, and that old cow who had tried to nobble him was going the same way.

He returned to his desk and dialled the number of the local television station, to make sure that the result of the Ridget Inquiry made it on to the evening news.

130

Seventeen
Iffy Breaks the Rules

The Great Hagges had decided to give their students a night off. Drusilla had received a letter in the post from one of her nieces, who wrote that the Grim Ghoul of Grisley Deep was very unwell. He had always had problems with his stomach, which was sensitive, and now he was a mere shadow of his former self. The old mine workings at Grisley were not very far away and the Great Hagges felt it was their duty to help if they could. So Drusilla packed her special bag of tonics and remedies, Fredegonda oiled her thumb and Goneril backed the car out of the old stables and gave it a rub-down. Before they left, Fredegonda gathered the ghosts in the courtyard, and addressed them.

'We will be away for the night. As responsible phantoms, I am sure you do not need to be told to respect the regulations of this establishment. However, I would like to remind you that if Mountwood is to continue its important work unmolested, we must not create any disturbance in the local community. Vicar Flitch down the road at St Agnes has on several occasions in the past thought about coming here to exorcize Mr Crawe. Imagine how excited he would be if he found out about all of you. So a quiet period mulling over your work and rejuvenating tired ectoplasm is the order of the night.'

With that she climbed into the front seat beside Goneril and the Rolls disappeared up the track to the main road, its headlamps cutting a fine swathe through the shadowy fir trees.

For a while after the Hagges had left the ghosts flitted quietly about, feeling relaxed and sort of holidayish.

The Phantom Welder appeared here and there and said, 'Boo! How was that for scary?' until a legless Anglo-Saxon warrior from the Isle of Thanet told him to stop mucking about and leave him alone. Cousin Vera the Banshee drifted into the main hall and sat down on the edge of the well, dangling her spindly legs over the side. She had as usual a touch of the sniffles, and drops formed on the end of her nose and dripped steadily into the dark waters below. They didn't bother Angus Crawe, nor did her woeful monotonous voice.

Vera liked talking to Angus Crawe, mainly about how she would be bottom of the class at Mountwood, which she had known from the beginning because she had been bottom of the class all her life.

'I am a failure, you see, a banshee must wail, and I wail not. Or not very well, anyway.' Angus Crawe did her a lot of good. He never interrupted, he had no opinions, yet she was sure he understood. Sometimes, not very often, she paused to say, 'You see?' or 'Don't you agree?' and she always got a reply, if not a very clear one.

'Divn'na' or, 'Why aye, man,' or, 'Getaway wi'yus,' echoed from the depths. But it was enough for her to feel that someone cared.

The night wore on, and soon Vera was no longer

alone with Angus. One by one the ghosts glided into the hall, floating around rather aimlessly among the rafters or coasting along the walls. The truth was that they were bored. They had become so used to the strict timetable followed by the Great Hagges that when they suddenly had a lot of free time they didn't know what to do with themselves.

Vera spotted her cousin Iphigenia standing alone in a corner, and left the well-mouth to go over to her. 'Hello, dear. Where are Ron and Percy?'

'I really couldn't say.'

Vera was not much of a wailer, but she knew about worry and sadness, and she could tell straight away that things were not right. Soon Iphigenia had told her about her row with Ron over that foolish sprite.

'And now Ron is on the roof and won't come down, and Percy spends all his time in the byre, playing with the cat.'

At that moment they both saw Kylie starting to emerge through the wall beside them.

'Oh no!' whispered Iphigenia, and began to thin herself out, but it was too late.

'Excuse me, Mrs Peabody,' said Kylie. 'Could I have a word?

Iphigenia merely nodded.

'It's just ...' stammered Kylie. 'It's just that I wondered if I had done something to annoy you?'

'Of course not.'

'Oh good, because I did so want to ask you about my boils the other night. Were they all right, do you think?' And she smiled the little modest smile that means, 'Wasn't I brilliant?' Then she added, 'Though I'm sure you would have been much better.'

Iphigenia looked at her. That was exactly what she thought, but she wasn't going to say it. 'You made an impression on Miss Goneril, did you not?' she said instead. 'And all your fellow students. I suppose that was the idea.'

'I wanted to do my best.'

'And that was your best?'

'Well, I made as many boils as I could, you know. Like Miss Fredegonda said – more is better.'

'There is a difference between more and too much.'

'What do you mean?'

'Frankly, darling, you were a bit over the top. Rather a vacuous performance.'

This was not a nice thing to say to someone who was hollow and couldn't do anything about it. Fortunately Kylie wasn't sure what 'vacuous' meant. However, she knew perfectly well that Iphigenia was not being kind, and she came from a long line of Scandinavian spirits who had lured bear hunters and woodcutters to their deaths for generations, so spirit she had.

'You *are* annoyed, aren't you? I wonder why. Perhaps you can't stand that I did rather well,' she hissed.

By this time quite an audience had gathered round the two phantoms, who were staring at each other with undisguised fury.

'What's going on?' said the Phantom Welder.

'She says I'm no good. She's jealous,' screeched the sprite, pointing a long pale finger at Iphigenia.

134

'Not at all. If she's too brainless to understand—'

The Phantom Welder just had to put his oar in, and that was really the cause of what happened next.

'Oh, leave her alone, Mrs Peabody. She's only a slip of a thing. She does her best, and that should be good enough for anybody, I reckon.'

Iphigenia's ghostly eyes widened, her eyebrows arched, her nostrils quivered. She tossed her glorious head of burnished hair and in a voice that she had last used when playing the title role in *Antony and Cleopatra*, she turned to the Phantom Welder and said, 'And as for you, you think you're just wonderful, don't you? No need to question anything. You have your boiler suit, your silly welding torch, your pathetic excuses for jokes, your "I am a simple working man" attitude. You have your "I can tell right from wrong", your 'I don't get that arty stuff". So pleased with yourself. So complacent. Well, let me tell you something, Mr I-like-a-simple-fry-up-no-fancy-food-for-me. Haunting isn't a parlour game, a bit of a giggle. *True* haunting is high art. One must dig deep. One must tear down one's own narrow boundaries and stand alone. One must risk everything.'

'Crikey,' said the Phantom Welder.

'I am sick of this sham haunting,' Iphigenia went on, her voice rising in a crescendo. 'This pretending to be scared. Where's the real thing?'

Nobody spoke. Then a nervous stink wafted towards them, and the Druid said, 'Excuse me, but we can't do real haunting, can we? It is against the school rules, you know, the Law of Mountwood. The Law that goes . . .'

'From our fiery forefathers forthgiven
Rightly written of runewise relatives
Disturb not decisions, deeds and dictates,
Helpless and hope-broken be he hailed who high-
    handed
Lets loud-sung Law limply languish
Beating bold breasts . . .'

'Stop him, somebody!' cried a lady ghost from one of Britain's noblest families who had been starved to death by accident and had haunted the larder of her stately home ever since. It was Iphigenia who brought the Druid up short before he got into full flow; he could have gone on all night without stopping for breath. Why should a ghost breathe if he doesn't want to?

'Fiddlesticks, you soppy old man. "More is better"? Ha! I'm going out. Are you coming, Kylie darling? Or do you prefer to stay here and play "Boo" with Mr Simple Working Man here?'

With a violent swoosh, Iphigenia threw herself through the oaken door of Mountwood and vanished into the night.

Kylie's blood was up, in a manner of speaking. Iphigenia's words had stung. They had made her feel like a mincing teacher's pet, and she wasn't having any of that. If something was going to happen, she was going to be there. She swept out after Iphigenia.

At that moment Ron, who was getting tired of sulking on the roof, stuck his head through the ceiling and looked down.

'What's going on? Where's Iffy?'

The ghosts fluttered chattering around him,

telling him what had happened.

'Whoa, hold on. Are you telling me Iffy's gone out? In a temper? Breaking the rules? She can be a bit flighty sometimes. I blame myself. I could have stopped her. Perhaps,' he added.

The ghosts looked at him.

'We'll have to go out and find them,' said Ron. 'Nothing else for it.'

There *was* nothing else for it. The ghosts dematerialized and streamed invisibly out of Mountwood, following the tingly atmosphere that Iphigenia and Kylie had left like footprints in the ether. The last to leave was the fat housemaster, who was worried that he might be caned for breaking school rules. But even he, his chins wobbling, followed in the end.

Down in the village that nestled in the valley below Mountwood was a nice little pub called the Fox and Hen. A few local farm labourers and estate workers had gathered there as usual for a quiet pint and a game of darts. It was just before closing time, and the talk turned, as it quite often did, to Mountwood. Most of them avoided the place if they could. Rumours of Angus Crawe had been around for years and years, and recently funny noises had been heard that definitely weren't owls or foxes. Nobody would dream of going there at night. And since the arrival of the three retired ladies, they avoided it in daytime as well.

'Ugly as sin, they are,' said the postman, who was sitting in a corner by the fire. He had to go there to deliver letters, whether he wanted to or not. 'Back of a bus ain't in it. And scary too. Like you'd be turned into a frog or something if you rubbed them up the wrong way.'

The other occupants of the snuggery laughed.

Standing at the bar was a man called Vince Grafton. He wasn't a local. He lived in the nearby market town and worked, when he worked at all, in a garage. He always wore a donkey jacket, slicked-back hair and a sly look, and he fancied his chances with the ladies, although he was married. He treated his wife terribly. When he was at home, which wasn't very often, he was nasty to her, taking every chance he could to make her feel useless and ugly, although she wasn't, and shouting at her if he didn't like her cooking.

Now Vince finished his beer, thumped his glass down on the bar and said in a loud voice, 'Three old wrinklies and a funny noise? It doesn't take much to scare you lot.'

He took a greasy comb out of his back pocket and ran it through his hair. He wouldn't have minded an argument, or even a bit of a fight. He was that sort. But nobody in the room could be bothered. They just looked at each other and shrugged their shoulders. People in country villages very rarely fight with people they don't know.

Vince laughed, went out to the car park and drove off into the night.

He took the narrow road that wound upward through the woods. Rounding a sharp bend, his headlights picked out a pale figure standing at the side of the road. As he got closer, he saw that it was a woman with a mass of auburn hair; she was wearing a long, old-fashioned dress. She must have been stranded on her way to a party, thought Vince. Maybe her car had broken down.

Normally he would not have stopped to help. He had never helped anyone in his life. But as he slowed down for a better look, he burst out, 'You're in luck, Vince, my boy.'

She was a real stunner. Ten out of ten.

Vince stopped the car and looked at himself in the rear-view mirror. Irresistible, that's what he was. Looked like a film star. He leaned over and opened the near-side window. 'Need a lift, pet?'

Iphigenia (for it was she) gave him the most endearing smile imaginable.

'Oh, thank you so much. I am quite lost and alone.'

'Are you now?' Better and better, thought Vince. 'Hop in then.'

The beautiful woman said something under her breath, and then seemed almost to float towards the car. She got into the passenger seat. The words that Vince hadn't caught had been directed to Kylie, who had melted into a tree close by.

'Come along, darling, watch and learn.'

Vince put the car into gear and drove on, out of the dark woods and on to open moorland. A thin fingernail of crescent moon rode the night sky, not bright enough to dull the stars whose soft light bathed the heather in an eerie glow.

'Oh my,' simpered Iphigenia. 'It is wild up here.'

'It's wild all right,' said Vince.

High up on the moors, where you could see right across to the dark ridge that scarred the horizon on the other side of the valley, Vince pulled off the road and stopped the car.

'Why are you stopping?'

Vince grinned his wolfish grin. 'To enjoy the view, you know.' He reached into the pocket of his jacket and took out a bottle of vodka. He unscrewed the top and took a swig. 'That's better. Here you go. Should warm you up a bit.'

'No, thank you.'

Vince's next trick was to tell a spooky story, so that she would squeak a bit and cuddle up to him. 'See that big rock up there? That's Gibbet Rock, where they used to hang the border reivers, when they could catch them.'

'Ooh,' said Iphigenia, trying to sound frightened. Vince was talking rubbish. Gibbet Rock was a mile farther down the road, as she knew very well. She had met some of the hanged criminals only the other night. They were mates of Angus Crawe and had popped in to have a little natter at the bottom of the well.

'And then there was Mad Meg,' Vince went on, 'She was going to be burned at the stake for a witch, but she pulled a knife out of her sleeve and slit her own throat before they could light the pyre.'

This was complete nonsense. Vince was making the whole thing up.

'How interesting.' Suddenly Iphigenia's voice had changed. It was a chilling, toneless whisper.

Vince looked at her in surprise. She sat there smiling as before, her beautiful face framed by her marvellous hair, but her eyes ... there were two blank staring white holes where those soulful eyes had been. The hair rose on the back of Vince's neck.

'Was it a knife like this?' Iphigenia asked in the

same frozen whisper, and from her sleeve she drew a dagger. Dark red liquid dripped from the blade. Still smiling the same empty-eyed smile, she stuck the point into her neck just below the ear and drew the blade across her own throat. A thin line of blood oozed from the wound and ran down her neck. She spoke again. 'It's cold on the moors of a night. Won't you join me?'

In a spasm of horror Vince lashed out. His fist passed right through Iphigenia, who was rapidly fading.

'We'll meet again.'

Her voice was barely audible now. It seemed no more than a wind soughing across the heather. 'Remember me, Poor Meg o' the Moor, remember me . . .'

Vince forced the car into gear and drove off like a madman. His hands were shaking so badly he could hardly hold the wheel. He drove at breakneck speed, skidding around bends with his foot on the floor. He didn't slow down until he was back in the valley among the trees.

'Somebody must have drugged me,' he mumbled. 'What a total nightmare.'

Then he happened to glance in his rear-view mirror. Sitting on the back seat was Iphigenia, blood still running down her neck and covering her dress in an ever-widening stain. The same eyeless smile was on her face.

'I'll never leave you, my dear one,' she whispered. 'I'm yours forever.'

It was too much. Vince screamed and collapsed over the steering wheel. Out of control, the car careered off the road and crashed into a tree. He was thrown clear and lay in a lifeless heap in the bracken a few yards from the wreck, his face set in a grimace of terror. His hair had gone completely white.

Kylie appeared on the back seat of the car beside Iphigenia, where she had been sitting all the time.

'Oh, Mrs Peabody, that was unbelievable. It was fabulous. I've never seen anything like it.'

Iphigenia smiled at her. 'It's technique, darling. It can be learned.'

'No, no, it's more than that. Inspired it was. And you hadn't even prepared.'

'Well, my love, one must be open to the moment. Improvisation is a skill too.'

Happily they glided out of the car together, all their past enmity forgotten. At that moment Ron Peabody's manly tones echoed through the night.

'Iffy! Iffy!'

All the ghosts swarmed out of the forest with Ron at their head. Everyone gathered around Vince's lifeless form.

'Will you look at that!' said the Legless Anglo-Saxon Warrior from the Isle of Thanet. He was not only without legs, he had no nose and a detached ear, so it was not always easy to judge his mood. But now it was clear he was impressed. 'That man's been scared to death. Haven't seen that for a while.'

There was huge excitement among the ghosts. Kylie told them all about the marvellous performance she had witnessed, and of course Iphigenia was heaped with praise. Everyone agreed that this was one in the eye for plastic Halloween masks and jolly jokey ghost cartoons.

They were chattering cheerfully, pointing out Vince's rigid terrified face ('That's what I call a Halloween mask,' said the Shortener, and everyone laughed and said how witty and clever he was), when they heard a car coming. The Phantom Welder instantly recognized the throaty hum of a perfectly engineered six-cylinder engine.

'That's the Rolls,' he said. 'We're toast.'

'Perhaps we should make ourselves scarce,' said the Shortener, putting on his bowler hat. The ghosts thinned out and scattered into the unseen as fast as they could.

Too fast. The starving duchess left her right foot behind, and the ear of the Legless Anglo-Saxon Warrior hung about just a bit too long. It got caught in the beams of the headlamps as the Rolls swung round the last bend.

Inside the car Fredegonda said, 'Stop! I know that ear.'

Goneril braked, and the Great Hagges could see Vince's car with its front end crumpled against a tree trunk and its rear wheels in the air. They could also make out the figure of Vince, lying like a discarded rag doll a little way off.

'An accident, oh dear,' said Drusilla, sitting up in the back seat where she had been resting. She had worked hard sorting out the mess that was the Grim Ghoul's digestive system and was rather tired.

'Accident? I have my doubts,' said Fredegonda grimly. Her thumb was pricking and tickling as it sometimes did when things were afoot. The Hagges got out of the car and walked towards Vince's body.

They stood looking down at the chalky horror-struck face.

'Well, well. Scared to death,' said Fredegonda.

'Unfortunately not. Only comatose, I'm afraid,' said Drusilla in a disappointed voice. She had already been having a number of little culinary ideas – roadkill is roadkill after all.

Fredegonda frowned. 'You would think,' she said, 'that one night off was not too much to ask. There has been a serious breach of discipline. There have been pranks; there have been high jinks. And they didn't even complete the job. What shall we do?'

'Shall we just finish him off and leave him?' suggested Goneril, looking around for a large stone.

'Quite impossible, I'm afraid. The police are terribly good at this kind of thing nowadays. They will work out that he didn't die in the crash and start poking around. Drusilla, can you come up with something?'

'I can bring him round, I think,' said Drusilla, and went back to the car.

She came back with a small phial, uncorked it and asked, 'Could you help me, Goneril dear?'

Goneril took hold of Vince's ankles and lifted him up so that he was hanging upside down from her outstretched arms, limp as a bin bag. Drusilla knelt down and poured a few drops from her phial into Vince's left nostril, counting carefully as she did so, 'One, two, three, and one for luck.'

Goneril put him down. Suddenly he spluttered, arched his back and then leaped to his feet, staring wildly around him and waving his arms.

'No . . . get off me . . . I won't . . . Aargh!' he howled.

They threw Vince on to the back seat of the Rolls

and drove off. While he babbled and screeched and wept, Drusilla went through his pockets.

'Vincent Grafton,' she said, after finding his driving licence and a couple of unpaid bills. 'Twenty-one Lavender Terrace, Matherley. He was obviously on his way home.'

After coasting quietly around the housing estates on the outskirts of Matherley, the Hagges found the right house.

Goneril got out of the car, fetched Vince from the back seat and tucked him under her arm. She walked up to the door of number twenty-one, dropped him on the front step, rang the bell and went back to the car.

The Great Hagges sat in silence for a while, watching. A light went on in an upstairs room, and a few seconds later the front door opened slowly. In the glow of the porch light they saw a woman, still young but with marks of weariness and despair on her face, bend over the huddled shape on her doorstep.

'Vince?' they heard her say.

Vince Grafton crept past her on all fours into the house. He never left it again. After a long time he recovered slightly. He learned to sew, and to cook healthy food, and he even found out where the vacuum cleaner was kept. His wife found a nice job in the library, and every day she locked him in carefully before leaving the house. He insisted on it. Sometimes on a Sunday she suggested a little stroll by the river. But Vincent always refused, trembling in every limb.

'Not going out there,' he said. 'Meg's out there.'

Eighteen
The Markham Street March

Daniel and Charlotte were in Daniel's attic room, sitting on the low windowsill.

They had lost. The results of the inquiry had been announced, with articles in the newspaper and reports on the local news station. Work would start soon in the park, and in a month or two the demolition of Markham Street would begin.

Rain was falling in a steady determined way, as though to say that it had got into its stride and wasn't planning on letting up any time soon. It drummed on the roof slates and gurgled in the guttering. Now and then, when a gust of wind shook the leaves of the chestnut tree on the other side of the street, it smattered against the windowpane.

'The Bennetts are moving tomorrow; I met Gillian on the way home from school,' said Charlotte.

'I heard.'

'How about you?'

'I think we'll go to that place on Wellington Road. My dad says that the compensation money should be enough. At least he'll have a bit of garden out the back.'

I can't believe it's over, Daniel. I just can't.' Charlotte leaned her forehead against the windowpane.

'It isn't over, Charlie. Not until they swing a wrecking ball through our front door.'

'I get the Hector thing, Daniel, I really do. But this is real. It's not an old story about Helen of Troy.'

'Come on, Charlotte. You're Boudicca, remember. What are we going to do now?'

Mrs Wilder was wondering the same thing.

Jessie and Mr Jaros had come over for a cup of tea. Jessie had struggled up the stairs to the big room on the first floor and flopped gratefully down in front of the gas fire, where she instantly fell asleep. Mrs Wilder and Mr Jaros sat opposite each other in comfortable chairs, and while Mr Jaros nibbled silently on his biscuit, and the rain pattered on the windows, Mrs Wilder considered the situation.

She didn't feel like giving up quite yet. A small modern flat somewhere in the suburbs had not been part of her plans at all. She had planned on dying in her own bed, or preferably at her desk, in Markham Street, with Karin to arrange the flowers and Peter Richards playing some Schubert with a few friends from the orchestra. And that sweet girl Charlotte, who really had a lovely speaking voice, could do the reading. They were all so kind and thoughtful in that peaceful way that never made you feel as though they were doing you a favour. She had found a home in Markham Street, and although they would never know it, for she would never tell them, they had mended her heart, the heart that was broken so very many years ago when she climbed on to that train, with a number on a label round her neck, and waved goodbye to her parents.

She had been Lottie Weissman then, a nine-year-old girl from Austria, and all she had when she came

147

to England was a small cardboard suitcase and the address of one of her father's friends, stitched on to the inside of her coat. She hadn't known then how bad it would be. Being sent away from her parents was painful enough, but the worst of it, the whole truth, came out later. Her mother and father had been swept away by the horrible war that followed, and were gone forever.

She had worked hard at making a good life and becoming a writer; she was grateful for her escape, and grateful to her new country for making it possible. But it wasn't until she settled in Markham Street that she found again the feeling of having a real home. Mrs Wilder knew, more than anyone else on the street, what they were fighting for. Not just for some nice old houses, but for the place where they belonged. Home.

'You know, Fjodor,' she said aloud, 'we really shouldn't let that Bluffit man get away with this. The whole of City Hall seems to do what he says. I have been talking to Sam Norton, who wrote that article. He's been digging around and he says that there was some kind of a deal between Bluffit and that buffoon Ridget – a housing scheme on Ridget's estate that he wanted stopped. But he can't prove it. Or not yet, anyway. We should give him all the help we can. If he can show that the whole inquiry was a farce, then they will at least have to reopen it.'

Mr Jaros was in a deep Central European gloom. 'Help him? How can we help him? We are crushed by the forces of capital. We are downtrodden.' In his younger days Mr Jaros had been a bit of a firebrand, but things had happened to him in

Prague that had dampened his fervour.

'Time, Fjodor, time. Sam Norton needs time. We must frighten the politicians. They are the ones who decide in the end, and they are always terrified of people not voting for them. That's all they care about. Most of the time they do what Bluffit wants, but if they think that people might not vote for them, they will do anything.'

And so the plans were laid for the Markham Street March.

Mrs Wilder invited everybody over the next day, and Karin Hughes brought huge amounts of cinnamon buns. She had, she said, made far too many. It was something that happened to her sometimes when she was sad and homesick.

While they chewed, Mrs Wilder told them about Sam Norton and read out a declaration that she had written, saying that there was corruption in high places, and that the council members of all parties were abusing the rights of the citizens by not doing something about it. Everybody signed it, and then Daniel and Charlotte spent the whole afternoon trudging round the neighbourhood knocking on doors and getting as many signatures as possible. They got very wet and cold, because although it was early summer they were in England, and the grey skies that hung above them like a damp woollen blanket had still not wrung themselves dry.

At last the rain got bored and moved on to soak the Lake District instead. The day of the march dawned chilly but clear.

There were not very many of them; some of the residents of Markham Street had already decided to take their compensation money and move. But there were one or two people from other streets close by the park. The Patels from the corner shop opposite the park joined them. Their business was finished if the plans went through. Daniel's parents greeted them and they walked along together.

Charlotte's mother had stayed at home with Alexander and the baby, but Jonathan and George had come along on their bicycles. Daniel and his friend Mike had made some placards in Daniel's father's allotment shed, and Charlotte had painted slogans on them, saying 'Save Markham Street' and 'Big Business is Bad Business' and 'Bluffit is Bent'.

She had done one saying 'Ridget is a Nitwit', but Jim Dawson had said that they shouldn't use it, because it wasn't Ridget's fault he was an idiot.

'I mean, you don't go around mocking slugs because they don't know their seven times table, do you?' he said, and Charlotte had to admit that there was some justice in this. The writing was a bit wonky in places, because Charlotte had had quite a lot of help from Jonathan and George, but the placards made it seem like a proper protest march, and not just a crowd of people on their way to a match (Mike was wearing his football scarf).

They headed off towards City Hall. It wasn't really freezing, more brisk, but Mrs Wilder was taking no risks with her circulation, and she was properly muffled up. She had her astrakhan hat on, and her long winter coat, and looked quite fierce and determined Inside each of her woollen gloves she carried a small

150

round stone that Karin Hughes had heated up in the oven before they set off.

'That was how we kept our hands warm when we walked to school in winter,' Karin had told her.

They didn't walk very fast, and to everyone's surprise they were soon caught up by the Bosse-Lynches.

Mr Bosse-Lynch was wearing his business suit and a club tie, and Mrs Bosse-Lynch had a hat on and a string of pearls and looked a bit like the queen. Peter Richards walked beside them for a while.

'Good of you to come,' he said.

'Well, we don't want them thinking that Markham Street is only inhabited by eccentrics and . . .' Mrs Bosse-Lynch hesitated, looking down her nose at Peter, 'Odd people.'

'No indeed.'

There was quite a long way to go – too far for Mrs Wilder really, who struggled a bit towards the end and did the last bit with her hand on Daniel's shoulder – but at last they reached the imposing entrance of City Hall.

Jack Bluffit looked down from the window of his office at the crowd gathering on the steps below.

'What a bunch. Not many of them, are there?'

'No, sir,' Snyder replied.

'Have you called the commissioner?'

'Yes, sir. He is sending a police officer.'

'*A* police officer? One? What good is that? I want the riot squad. Knock some heads together and send them home.'

'He seemed to think that was unnecessary, sir. He mentioned the right of peaceful protest.'

'Stuff the right of peaceful protest. Get him on the phone.'

But just then the phone began to ring.

'That'll be him,' said Bluffit. 'Out of the way. I'll take it.'

He snatched up the receiver. As he listened, his face changed to a furious scowl and his mouth set in a grim line.

'Yes, I got that,' he muttered at last, and slammed the receiver down again. 'That, Snyder, was the council chairman,' he snarled. 'Now I have to go down. I told you to fend him off, tell him I wasn't in.'

'Well, sir,' replied Frederik smoothly, 'you picked up . . .'

'Oh, be quiet, clever clogs. An assistant is supposed to assist.'

Bluffit stormed out, slamming the door behind him. He didn't see Frederik Snyder sticking his tongue out at him behind his back.

He emerged on the steps of City Hall looking less furious. He knew that there would be reporters there. That rat-faced creep Norton wouldn't miss a chance like this.

He had taken some deep breaths in the lift and forced his face into what he thought was a smile, although in fact he looked as though he had just come from a rather painful session at the dentist.

As he appeared the protesters struck up a chant that Jim Dawson had composed.

'Hey, hey, Mister J, how many homes have you wrecked today?'

Bluffit held up a meaty hand, and the chant faded

away. 'Citizens, what can I do for you?'

He glanced to one side and twisted the corners of his mouth up even more as a photographer from the local paper raised his camera.

Mr Jaros stepped forward and walked up the steps towards Jack Bluffit. He looked very distinguished, with his mane of silver hair and his dark intelligent eyes. He had borrowed his jacket back from Jessie, brushed off the hairs and ironed it, so he was wearing a whole suit.

'We are here to protest against the destruction of our homes and demand an investigation into the conduct of the inquiry. We wish to present this petition to the chairman of the county council.'

Mr Jaros looked every inch the English gentleman, and could easily have been mistaken for the Honourable Somebody or even Sir So-and-So. But he was very nervous, and his normally perfect English let him down. He said 'vee' instead of 'we' and 'vish' instead of 'wish'.

Jack Bluffit looked at him, and stopped pretending to smile.

'Don't get your hopes up,' he said. 'It's all legal, and in this country we obey the law. Any true Englishman would know that.'

From the grown-ups in the crowd there was a sharp intake of breath. Peter and Jim exchanged looks.

'I don't believe it,' said Peter.

Mrs Wilder was fairly deaf, but Bluffit had a loud voice and she hadn't missed a word. 'Is there no morsel of decency in that man?' Daniel heard her say, and he turned to look at her. He saw her take off her right glove, and in her hand was a small stone. With all her strength she hurled the stone at Jack Bluffit.

All her strength was not very much. The stone flew in a gentle curve and bounced harmlessly off Bluffit's well-filled waistcoat.

This time the smile that spread over Bluffit's features was not the strained mask he had put on for the reporters' cameras. It was a real beaming smile of satisfaction. He pointed at Mrs Wilder and shouted at the policeman who was standing quietly on the other side of the street:

'Arrest that woman. She is violent and dangerous!'

The policeman had to do something now, so he stuffed the remains of his lunch sandwich in a waste bin and advanced towards the crowd.

'Don't worry, Mrs Wilder. We will cover you with our bodies,' cried Jim, who had enjoyed a game of rugby at university and sometimes missed it badly.

'Oh please, I'd rather not,' said Mrs Wilder.

She was feeling rather frail and didn't want to be covered in bodies. She had been completely enraged by Bluffit's foulness to Mr Jaros, but now she just felt old and tired. 'What can they do to me?' she said. And she walked through the crowd to meet the policeman.

Nineteen
Bonding

When the Great Hagges finally arrived back at Mountwood, a faint glow in the east was dousing the stars one by one and the moon was setting. They strode into the hall, and Fredegonda immediately rang the bell for assembly.

The Hagges took up their places, with their arms crossed, looking very grim. Slowly the hall filled up with wobbly spectres.

'I won't waste time here,' announced Fredegonda. 'We want the details, and we want them now.'

Her voice rang like cold iron. She was calm – a stern self-discipline was one of her strong points – but if the assembled ghosts had known how powerfully her thumb was throbbing and how close she was to losing her temper, then they would have been even wobblier.

Then Kylie, very quietly, said, 'It was my fault.'

The Phantom Welder found his voice. 'No, it wasn't. It was me and my big mouth again.'

Ron Peabody moved forward and stood to attention. His eyeballs jittered about quite alarmingly, but his voice was firm. 'Not at all, ma'am,' he barked. 'I claim full responsibility. I have been derelict in my duties as a husband . . . er . . .' His voice trailed off. He had put his foot in it again.

'As a husband?' Fredegonda's voice was bleak as

the Arctic tundra. 'Mrs Peabody? This is unexpected.'

Iphigenia glided forward. 'I was led by my artistic nature into a creative moment that I now realize I may have cause to regret. Mea culpa. No blame attaches to any other.'

Eventually the whole story came out. It usually does in the end, especially in the hands of such experienced questioners as the Great Hagges.

At last, after a short conference with her colleagues, Fredegonda declared, 'Mrs Peabody's offence is serious enough to justify expulsion from Mountwood. However, she was clearly provoked, and others must bear their part of the blame. We will announce our decision tomorrow night.' And the Great Hagges turned and marched off to bed.

Later, as they lay in their four-poster bed finishing off the last of their hot drink, Goneril chuckled. 'I do believe we're almost there.'

'Oh yes,' agreed Drusilla. 'We might have done it, my dears; we might just have done it.'

'The bonding – did you observe the bonding, Fred . . . Fredegonda?'

Goneril was feeling so pleased that she almost said 'Freddie', but she had called Fredegonda 'Freddie' once before, and had decided then and there that she would never, ever do so again.

'Of course I observed it,' said Fredegonda. 'Team loyalty, carrying the can, unmistakable. And Mrs Peabody . . . well, we knew she had it in her, but to see one's work pay off so handsomely, what a jolly fine thing.'

'And the others not far behind, in my view.'

'No indeed, my dear.'

When a class finally comes together as a unit, when the whole becomes more than the sum of its parts, that is one of the finest moments in a teacher's life.

Wearing something very close to beatific smiles, the Great Hagges fell asleep. Their rumbling snores pounded rhythmically through the old stones of Mountwood Castle.

PART THREE

Twenty
In the Nick

The day after the march Daniel and Charlotte sat on General Markham's pedestal and looked out over the city. The school holidays had started, and just so that every child in the city would be extra pleased, the weather had turned glorious. The sun shone from a cloudless sky, the stone plinth they sat on was warm, and for once the air was swept so clean that they could make out tiny flashes of white from the backs of the gulls as they circled and screamed down at the quayside.

'It just makes things worse,' said Daniel.

Charlotte understood what he meant. Somehow it would have been easier if it had been one of those dank, dark, dripping November days that smelled of rotting leaves and dog poo, with empty hamburger cartons and old newspapers flapping around your feet. But instead, this lovely day.

On a day like this Markham Park looked almost beautiful, with its bright beds of pansies and snapdragons. A line of fluffy ducklings teetered across the path behind their mother, who proudly waddled towards the pond saying *waap waap*, to concentrate their minds.

Already men in hard hats had turned up in a van and were walking about studying plans and pointing things out to each other. Any day now the heavy machinery would move in, and by the autumn Daniel and Charlotte would be living on opposite sides of a city of a million people.

And Mrs Wilder was still in the police station.

They were going with Mrs Hughes to visit her in the afternoon. Daniel's father said he didn't think she'd be there for long. The whole thing was ridiculous; she should just have been told off. But they might have to charge her with something because of all the fuss.

'All the fuss' was Jack Bluffit's work.

Bluffit had recognized the old lady who had thrown the stone at him. She was the one who had tried to make him look a fool at the inquiry, and now he saw his chance to get his revenge. He rang the newspapers, especially the ones that didn't mind printing rubbish as long as they sold a lot of copies, and the next day one of them ran a big headline saying 'Pensioner Assaults Head of Planning', and the rival newspaper went for 'Hooligans Besiege City Hall'.

Bluffit had made sure that he was quoted in both as saying, 'Democracy in this country is being undermined by violent urban terrorism.'

The whole point of the demonstration was forgotten.

Daniel and Charlotte walked back through the park.

'This might be the last time,' Charlotte said quietly.

Daniel was angry with her for saying it. That was the trouble with Charlotte; she always said what she was thinking, she always told the truth, and she always looked the world straight in the face.

Sometimes it was better to tell yourself stories, wasn't it? Even if deep down you knew that's what they were – just stories.

'We can go on fighting. You said we should; now you're the one who's giving up.'

'That's not fair. All roads end somewhere.'

'If we were real fighters we would just be starting. We would lie down in front of the bulldozers, and if that didn't work we would make bombs and blow them up.'

'I can't do that, Daniel. That's how innocent people die. That's how mothers lose their children and husbands lose their wives.'

No more was said until they turned in at Mrs Hughes's gate. She was sitting waiting for them in her front garden.

The gardens of Markham Street were small patches of ground, cramped as only urban gardens can be, but Karin Hughes's garden was a tiny little paradise. Roses and azaleas against the wall of the house, greedy for warmth from the brickwork, and in front of them the shy cyclamens and anemones, the phlox and pansies and mallow and cranesbill. And of course the herbs. There was even a small tree. Not just any tree. It was a silver birch, the first thing she had planted when she came to Markham Street, when waves of homesickness for the country of her birth still engulfed her from time to time. Now she sat in its dappled shade, as she had sat many times since the letter came, saying goodbye to its delicate foliage and gracious, slender lines.

She got up when she saw Daniel and Charlotte.

'Hello, shall we be off then?'

163

She sounded cheerful, but her face said something else. Had she been crying? Charlotte wasn't sure.

They went in the Hugheses' car to the police station. Mrs Hughes had filled a large basket with all sorts of things: a thermos of hot tea, home-made bread, a pot of her absolutely most special gooseberry-and-rhubarb jam, a Wensleydale cheese that she knew Lottie Wilder was particularly fond of and a very thick book that would take a long time to read. Daniel had a woollen blanket to carry, and Charlotte had the hot-water bottles, the pillow and the bedsocks. They walked up to the front desk. The sergeant behind the desk looked them up and down.

'How can I help you?'

'We are here to visit Mrs Wilder.'

'Visit? You can't just come in and visit her.'

'We can. I know we can. My husband talked to a lawyer. She has rights—'

'Well, just visiting is not on, and there's an end to it. You must take her home. This isn't a blooming hotel; it's a lock-up.'

'I don't understand. Is she free to go?'

'Of course she's free to go. I doubt if they'll even press charges.'

'But Mr Bluffit—'

'Now you listen here, madam,' said the police sergeant sternly. 'That Mr Bluffit might be the bee's knees over at City Hall, but his writ doesn't run here, and never will as long as I'm around.'

'But why is she still here?' asked Daniel.

'Ask her yourself,' the sergeant said, and came around his counter to lead them through to the cells.

Mrs Wilder spoke before the cell door was even open.

'Please go away; I simply cannot abide this constant disturbance. Oh, it's you Karin, and Daniel and Charlotte. How nice.'

'Are you all right?' Mrs Hughes said doubtfully. 'We brought you some tea and a few things.'

'How very kind. But I've just had a cuppa. That nice duty officer came in with it a little while ago. That's why I was a bit shirty when I thought he was back again. Isn't this amazing?' she went on. 'Banged up at my age. In the nick at last.'

'But, Lottie, they say you are free to go. We came in the car; we can take you home.'

'Oh, not you too, Karin. I've explained several times that I need a few more hours of peace to finish my notes, and then perhaps a little rest. I might leave tomorrow. This is ideal, you know. I was having such a difficult time with my book, and now when I have a chance to get the proper criminal atmosphere, everybody just wants to snatch it away.'

'You mean you want to stay in prison?' said Charlotte.

'Well, not forever, dearest, obviously. But if they put me in here, they can jolly well wait until I'm ready to go. Thank you for the lovely basket and the other things, and now you'd better be off. And please make sure they lock the door properly. It's that shut-in feeling I'm after. Such a special experience.'

They trooped out, making sure that the cell door shut with a satisfying clang behind them.

When they gathered again at the front desk the

police sergeant looked up. 'You couldn't budge her either? What a business.'

'But can't you make her go?'

'What, you mean arrest her and throw her into jail?' And he laughed bitterly at his own joke.

'She's writing a book,' said Charlotte. 'That's why she wants to stay.'

'A book, is it? So my lock-up is some kind of writer's retreat. What kind of book?'

'A detective story.'

'Hang on – Wilder. Is she Lottie Wilder? *The* Lottie Wilder?'

'Yes, she writes—'

'I know what she writes – great stuff.'

'You'll probably be in the next one.'

'You never! Think she'd sign a book for me?'

'I'm sure she would, but I'd let her get some work done first.'

'Of course, of course. But maybe another cuppa, and a biscuit . . . '

So they left, leaving the happy policeman chuckling to himself. 'Lottie Wilder, in my cells. That's something to tell the old woman.'

It was late afternoon when they got home. Daniel climbed the steps to his front door slowly. In Mrs Cranford's garden next door there was a huge pile of boxes, covered with a big sheet of plastic.

Mrs Cranford was clearing out her house. She was going to stay with her sister on the other side of the river, at least until she found somewhere of her own, and there would be no room for even half of her stuff. And her sister had a small terrier that conducted a personal and very angry war on every cat it met. So Tompkins's picture was in the newsagent's window and on the noticeboard in the local library: 'Gentle tabby seeks loving home to end his years in peace.'

So far there had been no takers. Mrs Cranford knew what came next. Perhaps Tompkins knew too, because he was lying on the on top of the pile of boxes with his chin in his paws.

When Daniel entered the house he heard voices from the front room, or rather a voice – Great-Aunt Joyce's. She was the only resident of Markham Street who was pleased about what was happening to them, and now, without really meaning to, Daniel found himself eavesdropping.

'One has to admit,' Great-Aunt Joyce was saying, 'that Mr Bluffit has a point. These old houses really are falling apart. Think how much easier it will be for me with fewer stairs to climb. I will be closer to the kitchen, Sarah, and you will not have so far to go with my tray. Of course, in a smaller establishment Daniel will have to contain himself, be a bit less bumptious. In fact I have been giving that some thought. Have you ever considered boarding school, John? A bit of discipline would do the boy some good. And you would have less trouble with him.'

Daniel's father wasn't a particularly talkative person, more of a doer. But now Daniel heard him speak.

'We have no trouble with Daniel, Aunt Joyce. And he will never, ever be sent away to school, even if we could afford it.'

'Well, I must say, even if it requires some scrimping and saving, I think you should show me some

167

consideration. The new place is much smaller, and I can't have him on top of me all the time.'

Then Daniel heard a chair being pushed back, and footsteps approaching the living-room door. He leaped up the stairs two at a time and reached the landing as his father came out into the hall below. Daniel looked over the banisters. He saw his father lift both hands to his head, grab two handfuls of hair and raise his eyes to the ceiling. He heard him groan, 'Oh, God help me, what am I going to do?'

He saw his father go to the front door, pick up his gardening shoes and leave the house.

Twenty-one
Drainpipe and Rolling Pin

Sleep would not come. Seeing your father or your mother in despair and not being able to do anything about it is one of the worst things that can happen to anyone. Perhaps *the* worst. Daniel would much rather have been run over by a train, or had his arm chopped off.

Time ticked slowly by. Daniel cried, and hit his head on the pillow, and got up to walk around, thumping his feet loudly to disturb Great-Aunt Joyce, and crept back into bed again and pulled the blankets over his head. Soon Markham Street would be a ghost town, with boarded-up windows and overgrown gardens and litter in the street, waiting emptily for the end.

A ghost town . . . Suddenly Daniel sat up in bed. The room was dark, and he remembered vividly that sobbing noise behind the wall and the arrival of Percy. He remembered something else too, a quiet voice speaking out of the darkness. 'I shall be in your debt until the end of time. If we can ever be of help . . . I mean it, I do.'

Daniel jumped out of bed. If ever anybody needed help, he needed it now. He had to speak to Charlotte, and it couldn't wait.

He rushed downstairs. He didn't need to turn the lights on; he knew every creaky floorboard and wobbly banister in the house. In the hall he pushed his feet into a pair of trainers and let himself out.

Under the street lamps Markham Street was silent. Daniel crossed over and ran down the street and round the corner, doubling back up the alleyway full of dustbins at the back of the row of houses. Charlotte had a room at the back, quite high up. When he got to her house, he stood looking up. It was almost too dark to see, but a big city is never really dark.

No light showed in Charlotte's window. He tried whistling. No response. He had a look at the sheer brick wall. There was an old drainpipe that showed definite possibilities. He had tried it once on his own house. He seemed to recall that it hadn't gone very well that time, but this time he would do it.

He started shinning up the drainpipe, bracing his feet against the wall. Luckily it had been put there by builders who cared about their reputations, and it was bolted firmly in place. At last he reached the level of Charlotte's window, and that was when he remembered quite clearly what had gone wrong last time. The windowsill was off to his right and he couldn't reach it.

'Charlie,' he hissed, 'wake up, please.'

No movement from Charlotte's room, no light. Daniel's legs were beginning to tremble with the strain of staying where he was. He put his head back and yowled. There were always stray cats having fights in the back alley, and Charlotte used to complain that they woke her up and she had to get up and throw water over them. Sure enough, a light went on in Charlotte's room, the sash window was pushed up and a tousled head appeared, followed by a hand holding a water jug.

'Charlie, it's me; it's Daniel.'

'Daniel? What on earth? What's happened? What's wrong?'

'I'm stuck.'

'Why are you here?'

'I won't be here much longer if you don't help me.'

'OK, hang on.'

'What do you think I'm doing?'

Charlotte disappeared. She was gone for what seemed to Daniel like a very long time. When she reappeared at last she had something in her hand.

'What's that?'

'A rolling pin.'

'A what?'

'A rolling pin. I had to go down and get it from the kitchen. I've tied some washing line round the middle. Try to grab it and sit on it – you know, like a swing. I've tied the other end to the bed leg.'

'Will it hold?'

'I have no idea. Why didn't you just ring the bell, for heaven's sake?'

Daniel didn't answer; he was trying to push the rolling-pin between his legs with one hand and keep his grip on the drainpipe with the other. He succeeded just in time, lost his grip on the drainpipe, swung down under the windowsill, scraping his knees in the process, and with a lot of pulling from Charlotte, fell into the room.

When he had got his breath back he got straight to the point, walking up and down the room while Charlotte retired to bed, hugging her knees and listening.

'We can't blow them up, we can't shoot them, I know that. But what if we scare them off? The ghosts

171

at Mountwood, you know, all Percy's friends and relations, they can come here and haunt. They're supposed to be learning to be really terrifying, aren't they? Well, they must be pretty good at it by now. And Percy's mother said if we ever needed help, they'd help us. Well, we do need help; we really do. We have to go and ask them to come. Get dressed, now, Charlie, we can sneak off and get the first bus from the station, or hitchhike or something. We can be there by this evening.'

Charlotte was silent, her brown eyes gazing at Daniel and a frown on her face.

'No.'

'No? No? Is that what you have to say? It's our last chance, you must see that. I might as well die. Don't you know what this is doing to my mum and dad?'

Charlotte never spoke much about her own troubles, but she knew what the destruction of Markham Street was doing to her own family. Her mother hadn't said anything to her, but Charlotte knew how desperate she was about having to move. It hadn't been easy for her since Charlotte's father had left them. Markham Street and their shabby old house had been what held her together.

'Daniel, shut up and listen. It's a brilliant idea. It's our only hope. But I will not sneak off again like a thief in the night without telling my mother where I'm going. We must tell the truth.'

'They'll say it's all nonsense and stop us going if we start talking about ghosts and Hagges.'

'It'll be all right. Anyway, I am not going to run out on my mum without a word. You'd better go now. And please, Daniel, use the stairs.'

172

Twenty-two
Lunatics

Mr Salter was confused. His son had come down to breakfast with an expression on his face that Mr Salter was very familiar with. It meant that he had something to say and he was going to say it.

When Aunt Joyce had left the table to take her morning bath, which meant that nobody could use the bathroom for at least two hours, Daniel started to speak. But the more he spoke, the more confused John Salter became. He stopped clearing the table to listen more carefully to his son, but it just didn't seem to make any sense.

The fact is that Daniel had bottled out. It was all very well for Charlotte to get on her high horse about speaking the truth, but it was easier said than done. He just could not risk being forbidden to go. So he started off rather vaguely.

'Charlotte and I met some people when we were in Carlisle. Three important ladies. We want to go there again and ask them for help.'

'What kind of help, Daniel? I don't understand.'

'Well, they were retired, I think, but they had power.'

'Power? What sort of power?' said Mr Salter, scraping the remains of Aunt Joyce's wholegrain muesli into the compost bucket.

'Well . . . they were . . . um . . . powerful. They had

some very . . .' Daniel struggled for words, 'some very special students.'

'I don't see how students can stop a multi-million-pound development. You saw what happened to the demonstration. Daniel, it's a fine thing that you want to do all you can, but I'm afraid you will be terribly disappointed. I know it's boring, but parents are boring people and I have to say it. You will only end up even sadder, and I don't think I can stand that. But l tell you what – if you get me the number, I'll give these people a ring and find out more about them. Then we can decide.'

'You can't do that.'

'Why not?'

'They're not on the phone.'

When the doorbell rang an hour or so later, Daniel was in his room. He went out on to the landing and heard his father open the front door and say, 'Oh, hello, Margaret.'

It was Charlotte's mother. He couldn't hear what she said because she was standing out on the front step, but he caught his father's reply clearly enough.

'A lunatic? No, Margaret, you must be wrong. Charlotte is anything but a lunatic. But come in, please, and I'll put the kettle on.'

They went into the kitchen.

Any minute now, thought Daniel, and he was right.

'Daniel!' shouted Mr Salter from the kitchen doorway. 'Come down here. I want to talk to you.'

When Daniel came into the kitchen Charlotte's mother was sitting at the table, resting her forehead in one hand and clutching a mug of tea with the other. She looked tired, as she always did, but now a look of puzzlement and worry had been added to her weariness. She was still wearing her apron and had flour on her jumper.

'. . . so now she's gone over to Mrs Wilder's and is terribly upset,' she was saying. 'But honestly, I think all this trouble has gone to her head. Should I ring a child psychiatrist, John? I think she needs help.'

'Let's ask Daniel what he thinks,' said Mr Salter, looking at his son. 'I suspect he can enlighten us.'

So Daniel told his father the whole story. When he had finished, he looked at his father, and feeling tears starting to his eyes he said, 'You don't believe a word of it, do you? I told Charlotte that we should lie about it. I told her.'

'Daniel, first of all, you're right, it is impossible to believe you. But you knew that, didn't you? At least you and Charlotte are telling the same story. So you're probably not insane.'

'Just simple liars.'

'Daniel, you are both very unhappy about moving; you need to comfort yourselves; it's all perfectly understandable.'

The telephone rang.

Daniel's father went out into the hall. When he came back he said, 'That was Lottie Wilder. She wonders if we could come round.'

They walked round in silence to number eight. The door was open and they went straight up to Mrs Wilder's big room on the first floor. Charlotte was sitting in a chair by the window, staring out. She didn't turn her head when they came in.

175

'Hello, Lottie. You're out, I see,' said John Salter.

'Yes. They put a car thief in the cell next door last night. Fascinating. I came home this morning and found Charlotte sitting on the front steps. I think we should have a little chat.'

'I agree,' said Daniel's father. 'But it seems a shame to bother you with all this, Lottie.'

'No bother at all. And I have a guilty conscience. I was part of it all.'

So Mrs Wilder told them about crossword puzzles, and finding Mountwood.

When she was finished, Charlotte's mother burst out, 'But why didn't you tell me? I'm her mother!'

'There is a simple answer to that. Charlotte told me in confidence. I respected that.'

'But . . .'

'There are no buts in this case, I am afraid. I am not, and never will be, a tale-teller.' Now they saw the other Lottie Wilder, the one who wrote about hard-boiled detectives and had made mincemeat of Jack Bluffit at the inquiry.

Charlotte turned her head from the window and said bitterly, 'You wouldn't have believed me anyway. You don't believe me now.'

John Salter spoke. 'Lottie, this is all very well, but a tale of ghosts and Great Hagges and haunting school, I mean, surely you don't think . . .' He was suddenly uncertain.

'I shall tell you what I think,' said Mrs Wilder, 'and then of course as these children's parents you must make up your minds whether to let them go on their . . . quest.'

'In the first place,' she went on, leaning back in her

chair, 'have you considered what an odd thing it is to make all this up. As one who is interested in mysteries, I wonder how Daniel and Charlotte, quite out of the blue, got the idea that there *must* be a place, not too far from here, whose name bears a resemblance to the words "forest" and "hills", and then in fact went on to find such a place. Now that *would* be insane. Unless they had prior information. As to the question of whether they received that information from a small frightened ghost in a nightdress . . . well, now we come to my second point.'

She was quiet for a moment. Then in a different voice, more dreamily, she said, 'It's all forgotten now, beyond our ken. Human beings no longer believe in the Perilous Realm, and that, I might add, is perilous indeed. But some day, some quiet evening perhaps, when you are walking off your supper, or having a breath of fresh air on your balcony, or taking a short cut down some backstreet to your favourite cafe, there will be a lull in the traffic, a moment quiet enough to hear a few starlings settling down for the night, or a mouse skittering along the guttering; and in that little lull, you will see something out of the corner of your eye: a movement, a shape, a shadow. And you will sense a small door opening in your mind.'

Mrs Wilder sighed. 'And then you will have to decide whether to shut it, or keep it open. It's your choice, and yours alone.'

For quite a long time nobody said anything. John Salter was remembering one late evening down on his allotment, when he had been tying up his broad beans, and had been so sure that someone was watching him over the fence that he actually called out to him. But when he looked again, there was nobody there. He was the first to speak.

'You'd better go, I think. Any port in a storm. What do you say, Margaret?'

'Yes, yes. Charlotte's always known her own mind.'

Charlotte jumped out of her chair, gave Daniel an I-told-you-it-would-be-all-right grin and ran over to Mrs Wilder, gave her a huge hug and planted a kiss right on the top of her grey head.

'Silly girl,' said Mrs Wilder.

Mr Salter had a talk with his wife when he and Daniel got back from Mrs Wilder's. At first she didn't want to let Daniel go, but she saw that her husband had made up his mind. He was quite determined. He might not quite believe in ghosts, but he believed in Daniel, and that was enough. And once he got into that state, as Sarah very well knew, then there was nothing to be done. Daniel was exactly the same. But she absolutely insisted on driving them all the way there.

'But you can't come to the actual castle, Mum. They don't know you.'

Mrs Salter was about to say something, but she saw her husband shake his head.

'That will be fine, Sarah. I'll book a room for you in the village and you can wait for them there.' For Sarah Salter the thought of a peaceful night all on her own in a quiet inn was such bliss that she gave in at once.

'In that case they must have proper sandwiches and sleeping bags,' she said, trying unsuccessfully to sound as if she was in charge.

Twenty-three
Noses and Thumbs

Drusilla was splashing about happily in a mossy pool about half a mile from Mountwood. It lay in a marshy dell where one of the peat-brown burns that came off the moors had a chance to slow down and spread itself out a bit before tumbling on down to the valley floor. She was collecting frogspawn to make her very own variety of tapioca pudding for the Hagges' breakfast.

They usually breakfasted at around six in the evening, before the ghosts were astir, so that they could discuss the night ahead and get themselves organized. But Drusilla was an early riser, and there was nothing she liked better than to take a little walk on the hills in the slanting evening light and see what she could collect. She had taken off her shoes and socks and waded out into the pool. It was quite delicious to feel the marsh mud oozing up between her toes as she scooped spawn into her little bucket.

Work was going on apace at Mountwood. The Hagges had not told the students that they were secretly rather pleased about Iphigenia's little escapade. However, they had let them off with a stern warning, and the ghosts were so relieved that they worked even harder than before.

Only last night Drusilla had had a wonderful success. The Druid had finally achieved smell control. After weeks of effort, trying and failing and trying again, the breakthrough had come. He had turned up as usual for his special-needs class, accompanied by a swirling stench of dead fish and untreated sewage.

Drusilla had said, 'I think you are trying too hard. You must relax; don't fight it; it is your greatest asset. Your stink is also you – you must greet it as your friend. Say quietly to yourself, "I am one with my smell; I embrace it."'

The Druid closed his eyes, and repeated again and again, 'I am one with my smell; I embrace it.'

This went on for quite some time. Then Drusilla, who couldn't exactly *see* smells but always knew exactly what they were up to, noticed that the stench that had hung in a drifting cloud around the Druid was beginning to concentrate itself in the region of his stomach; his deathly pale face took on a sickly greenish tinge, and suddenly the stench was gone.

'Oh! You have mastered it. Congratulations.'

'I have!' cried the Druid joyfully. 'It is within me. My smell is within!'

'It is. Now, this might be asking too much, but if you could release it again . . .'

The Druid closed his eyes. Like an invisible snake striking with its deadly poisonous fangs, a viciously nauseating stink shot out of his stomach, and a cockroach that was going about its business on the wall opposite coughed once, scrabbled a little with its back legs and fell lifeless to the floor.

'A cockroach – well done indeed!' exclaimed Drusilla. 'Cockroaches can stand almost anything, you know.'

The Druid smiled a proud smile, and apparently without effort withdrew his odour back into himself.

*

Drusilla came back to the present. The sun's lower rim was already nudging the distant fells. To the east a bank of clouds was building.

'I should be getting back,' she said to herself.

She straightened up and started to wade back to where she had left her shoes and socks on a convenient rock. She had one muddy foot on the bank and one still in the water when she suddenly stopped dead. Her nose had twinged.

'Hmmm,' she said.

She left the pool and climbed the side of the little dell to catch the light airs off the moor that signalled the beginning of the evening breeze. She pointed her nose straight into the air, and sniffed.

'Well, well,' she murmured.

At breakfast, as Fredegonda and Goneril were spooning up the last of their tapioca pudding, Drusilla said, 'We will have visitors tonight.'

'Yes,' said Fredegonda, looking down at her thumb, which had swollen up slightly and started to blacken at the tip.

Her thumb was very good at keeping her informed about what was going on. Sometimes she thought it was almost too excitable, too keen to tell her things that she could perfectly well have found out for herself. But on the whole they got on very well together, and she was conscientious about attending to its needs. Like a faithful pet that one has cared for over the years, it had found its way to her heart, and if anything had happened to it she would have been very upset.

'Those children,' said Drusilla. 'I caught a distinct

181

whiff of the boy, and a hint of the girl too.'

'When do you expect them to be here?'

'Around midnight, I should think.'

'What a bother.'

'Just when things were beginning to settle down nicely. Shall I deal with it?' said Goneril hopefully. She felt the need to be up and about. She had always been the most sporty of the three.

'It is tempting, I agree,' replied Fredegonda, 'but children aren't as easy to get rid of as they used to be. The place will be crawling with police cars and do-gooders in no time. We'll just have to keep our heads down. Batten down the hatches.'

So when the students gathered as usual for evening assembly in the great lower chamber of Mountwood, they got a surprise.

'Tonight it will be necessary to take some evasive action,' announced Fredegonda. 'Mountwood is threatened by intruders. So absolute disappearance by eleven o'clock, please. No groans, no rattling or gnashing. And no stray ears,' she declared, fixing the Legless Anglo-Saxon Warrior with a piercing look. His ear went red.

The Shortener raised a shy hand. 'If I may say so, wouldn't it be better to frighten them off? We would all like to show what we can do.'

'It is nice to see you so keen,' replied Fredegonda. 'You show a fine spirit, all of you. However, in this particular case . . .' she paused, remembering how the two children who had brought Percy home sat calmly by the wall while a crowd of phantoms howled and screeched in the courtyard, '. . . it might prove quite a hard nut to crack.'

Mrs Salter stopped the car at the head of the track.

'Are you sure you want to do this? It's terribly dark.'

'Mum, we'll be fine. I've got a torch and it's not cold. See you tomorrow.'

Daniel and Charlotte had decided to arrive at Mountwood at around midnight, to have the best chance of meeting everybody and explaining everything. They picked their way down the rutted track by the light of Daniel's torch. During the evening the sky had become overcast, and now not a single star was to be seen. The night was as black as soot, the darkness so solid that you could almost reach out and touch it, but treading gingerly they came at last to the courtyard of Mountwood.

Daniel let the beam of his torch play over the castle's louring front. It picked out the iron-studded door and, to the side, the bell pull. Charlotte walked forward, reached up and pulled with all her strength. The clanging of the bell sounded shockingly loud. It echoed through the castle for ages. Nothing happened. The silence was total, so complete that it hissed in their ears.

'Can they have gone? Is it deserted?' whispered Charlotte. It was difficult not to whisper in that soundless nothingness.

'No, they were going to be here for a year at least. Try again.'

Charlotte pulled the bell again. Again the frightful clamour, followed by utter silence.

'What shall we do?'

'We can't give up. Let's get some sleep in the byre

and then see if the Great Hagges come out in the morning.'

Daniel and Charlotte had never been sure that the ghosts would help them. But that they would simply have disappeared – really disappeared – had never occurred to them. They found their way to the byre and forced open the warped, half-rotten door. The pile of old straw was still there. They made a sort of nest for themselves, unrolled their sleeping bags and crept into them. They lay there in the darkness, trying not to think of what the future held if their mission should fail.

Charlotte was finally drifting off into a worried sleep when she quite distinctly felt something walk across her legs.

'Oh no, a rat!' she exclaimed, sitting up.

She had nothing against rats and mice in principle, but having one walk over you – and this had felt like a big one – in the middle of the night is hard to take for anyone. Then she heard a sound that was quite unmistakable: a quiet, contented purring.

'Daniel, where's the torch?'

Daniel fumbled around, found it and turned it on. They saw a tortoiseshell kitten, curled up and resting peacefully in the space between their sleeping bags.

Twenty-four
The Terrifying Worms

When the clang of the doorbell echoed through Mountwood all the ghosts ignored it, as they had been told to do. They remained completely invisible, absorbing themselves into walls, floors and cupboards. Not a single rattle or gnash was to be heard.

Hours passed, very difficult ones for Percy. He desperately wanted to go out and see Samson but he just didn't dare. His mother and father had told him very firmly to be absolutely quiet, and he thought he could manage that bit, even if he did sometimes let out a little hiccup by mistake.

But what about those intruders? The Great Hagges hadn't said who they were. They might be the kind that are dangerous for ghosts. There might be a whole clutch of clergymen out there in the darkness with garlic and little black books. The druid had told some horrible story just the other night about how badly ghosts were treated in the old days. Then Percy had a terrible thought. What if the intruders were dangerous not to ghosts, but to cats? He simply had to go out and see that Samson was all right.

Trembling in every phantom limb, Percy eased his way through the wall of the castle into the courtyard and sneaked over to the byre. He was totally invisible and the night was black as pitch, but he sneaked anyway, just to be on the safe side.

He glided into the barn, and immediately saw Samson sleeping quietly on the straw. But to his utter horror he saw something else. Two great worms were lying on either side of him! Percy knew about great worms. He knew about the Lambton Worm that had lived in the well at Lambton Castle and got bigger and bigger until it had eaten all the sheep and cattle. There was a song about it that Angus Crawe's mates had sung when they were visiting him only the other week. Geordie Lambton had killed it in the end, not far from here, but could it have had children? These ones weren't as big as the Lambton Worm, but there were two of them.

Percy was shaking with fear, but he simply had to be brave. Samson's life was in danger. He had to frighten them off. He began to materialize, wishing he had listened more closely to the scary-noise lessons.

'Ooh-wooh,' he said.

The worms twisted and turned. Percy almost vanished in fright, but he took hold of himself and tried again.

'Ooh. Ooh-wooh.'

Now the two worms lifted their heads, and to Percy's utter horror and astonishment he saw not the evil worm heads with red eyes and venomous teeth that he had been expecting, but the heads of Daniel and Charlotte.

Percy panicked. 'Oh no, they're eating my friends! Stop! Help, help!' he screeched.

'Percy, is that you?' said Daniel.

'Yes, yes, I want to save you, but I don't know how!' The tears poured down his cheeks.

'You don't have to save us. We're fine,' said Charlotte, sitting up, 'and we're very pleased to see you. We thought you had all left.'

Charlotte and Daniel crept out of their sleeping bags. Percy saw at once that he had been a bit foolish, but it didn't matter. He was so very pleased to see them.

He introduced them to Samson, and asked them if they had come on a bus, and then he cried, 'Oh, I forgot. How could I? I should be invisible, and so should you. There are intruders.'

'I think we *are* the intruders, Percy,' said Charlotte. 'We know that the Great Hagges don't want you to talk to humans, but we just had to come. We are in trouble. We need help.' And she told him what was happening to Markham Street.

'My mama will want to help you, I know she will,' said Percy when she had finished, 'but I'm not so sure about—'

At that moment there was a mighty crash and the door of the barn flew open. Three dark figures stood silhouetted in the wide doorway. Behind them a dark red flush in the sky hinted at the coming of dawn.

The Great Hagges advanced on Daniel and Charlotte. Drusilla uncovered a lantern, which cast its flickering light around the byre, chasing shadows into corners and illuminating the faces of the two children. Daniel and Charlotte moved closer together, but they stood their ground. Daniel opened his mouth to speak, but there was no time.

'We do not usually bother with children,' said Fredegonda, 'but since you are clearly determined to bother *us*, it seems we will have to make an exception. Goneril, if you would be so kind.'

Goneril stepped forward. Her long eyebrow had formed itself into a V-shape above her nose, and her left eyeball had turned green. Daniel's feet suddenly felt icy cold. He tried to move, but he was rooted to the spot. He turned his head to look at Charlotte. She looked at him, and he saw real fear in her eyes.

'Daniel,' she whispered, 'I can't move.'

Then the heap of straw in which they were standing began to heave and writhe and rustle. Charlotte though of rats and worse, but there were no rats. The straw itself was alive; it roiled and twisted and great ropes of straw began to encircle Charlotte's and Daniel's legs, and waists, and arms. In no time at all two straw dolls were standing there. Their noses stuck out a bit, but nothing else.

When Goneril was finished, Fredegonda said, 'Well, that will do for now, but we are not out of the woods yet.'

'No,' said Drusilla. 'Someone will be expecting them back. But perhaps I can think of something. Memory loss is a bit unreliable. A sudden shock can jolt it. I would go for some kind of permanent brain damage.'

'What's wrong with a good old-fashioned fire?' said Goneril, who liked a bit of a blaze. 'Accidents do happen.'

Discussing possible solutions to their little problem, the Great Hagges returned to the castle. There was only an hour or two before dawn, so no time to waste. Percy had vanished in terror when the Hagges arrived and hung about in the rafters of the byre not daring to move. As soon as they left, he fled to find his father and mother.

'You will be pleased to hear,' announced Fredegonda, when the wraiths and phantoms of Mountwood had drifted in, in answer to their summons, 'that the intruders have been temporarily discouraged. They will be dealt with later. Meanwhile we have missed a night's work, but there is still time for a workout before sunrise. Goneril will lead a session of ectoplasmic callisthenics.'

Goneril took over. 'Right, students, three separate groups, please, heads to your right, limbs to your left, torsos in a ring in between.'

Nothing happened. The ghosts stayed where they were. Fredegonda looked out over the crowd. Nobody moved. Only a faint smell of sweaty socks betrayed that the Druid, in spite of his new-found mastery, had let the tension get the better of him.

Iphigenia Peabody separated herself from the group and glided forward. 'We wish to say something.'

'By all means,' said Fredegonda, but her voice held a warning note.

'My son Perceval tells me that these two intruders are the children who saved him, and that they have come here in dire need, seeking our help.'

'Go on.'

'We feel that to bale them and then send them home unheard is not fair and just—'

'Fair and just? Fair and just?' All Fredegonda's pent-up disgust welled up in her and spilled over. 'Is it fair and just to paint skeletons on T-shirts and write stories about soppy teenage witches who moon

189

about like film stars? To put green plastic trolls into fast-food cartons for toddlers to play with? I will hear no more of this nonsense. Return to the business in hand.'

'No.'

'No! No?'

For the first time for several hundred years Fredegonda was lost for words. Goneril stood open-mouthed, showing both her teeth, and Drusilla's eyebrow had almost disappeared into her hairline.

'We refuse. We are on strike. We will not be moved.'

Fredegonda found her voice. 'All of you?'

She looked around.

The legless Anglo-Saxon warrior, pinioned by her steely gaze, looked as though he might be about to weaken. But the Phantom Welder, who was floating close by, spoke to him in a quiet but determined voice. 'We have to stick together, comrade. Don't be a scab, mate. They can't break us if we hold the line.' And he started to sing softly, *'The worker's flag is deepest red, stained with the blood of martyrs dead . . .'*

Iphigenia spoke again. 'We only ask that you give them a hearing.'

There was a faint hissing noise, like the wind blowing through ripe barley, as the other ghosts agreed.

A long silence followed.

'Fredegonda, dear,' said Drusilla, 'perhaps under the circumstances—'

Fredegonda interrupted her. 'Goneril, fetch them, please.'

*

190

Daniel and Charlotte were led by Goneril into the great lower chamber of Mountwood, and the ghostly gathering parted to let them through. Wisps of straw clung to their clothes and stuck out of their hair. Charlotte's face was drawn and thin, all eyes and mouth. Daniel's square features were set, his jaw clenched and his chin up. Both of them were pale and freezing cold. There was no heating in Mountwood. The walls were damp and dripping, and the assembly hall was lit only by a few smoking torches and a handful of will-o'-the-wisps whom Drusilla had befriended in the marsh.

'We have been asked to let you speak,' said Fredegonda frostily when they came to a halt in front of her. 'So speak.'

Fredegonda, tall, gaunt and forbidding, was enough to make anyone unsure of herself, but the children collected their thoughts as best they could.

Daniel began. 'Our houses are about to be destroyed; we have tried everything. We need your help.'

'Why should we help you? What concern is it of ours?'

'Only fear can stop them,' said Charlotte. 'We thought . . . We thought that's what this was all about.' And she gestured around the gloomy chamber with its milling spectres.

'And so it is. But we would also be helping you and your families. It would be a good deed. That is *not* what this is all about.'

'But you would be helping those old houses too. Don't ghosts need old houses to haunt? And they're

191

going to make such a mess of Markham Park. It's been there for ages.'

There was a desperate appeal in Charlotte's voice. She didn't know it, but she had hit the spot. The Great Hagges were very much against mess. Drusilla was a Lifetime President of the Society for the Preservation of the British Heritage, and had kept up contact even in retirement.

Now she said, 'Markham Park? I think I heard something about that. There is a Head of Planning whom the members have been complaining about for years.'

'Jack Bluffit,' said Daniel.

'That's the chap. I knew the original Markham, you know – Sir Guy of March Hamlet he was then, of course. Very respectable, and had a firm hand with the serfs.'

'There is another thing,' said Daniel. Suddenly he felt that they might be getting somewhere. 'We thought your students might need a bit of practice. You know, like trainee teachers, or soldiers on an assault course.'

It was this last remark that clinched it. Ever since Mrs Peabody's little jaunt they had been discussing the need for a bit of fieldwork. 'The litmus test,' Fredegonda called it.

The Great Hagges exchanged glances, and then Fredegonda nodded.

'Very well. We agree to your request, assuming that there are volunteers for the task. I will not make helping human children obligatory, of that point I am quite adamant. So,' she declared, turning to her students, 'who wishes to be a part of this enterprise?'

A surge of spectres, squawking and shrieking, 'I'll go! . . . Me, I'll do it! . . . I'm on, count me in!' told her that she would have no difficulty in raising her squad.

'I assume you can organize billets,' said Goneril.

'Billets?'

'Yes, of course. Where are they going to stay?'

'But I thought—' Daniel began.

'I doubt that. You clearly did not think. Ghosts need somewhere to attach themselves. Occasionally you might meet a wanderer, like the Druid here, but for the most part ghosts don't just haunt, they haunt *places* – houses, castles, ruins, graveyards . . .'

'Aye, and wells,' boomed Angus Crawe, from the depths.

'Exactly. I should have thought that was obvious. So can you accommodate them?'

'Yes. Yes, we can, it won't be a problem,' said Daniel quickly, before Charlotte could get an attack of honesty and admit that it might well be a problem.

Once a decision had been made, Fredegonda did not hang about.

'In three days from now, at midnight,' she declared.

Twenty-five
Heavy Machinery

It started the day after they returned from Mountwood. Mike came round to Daniel's house, and when Daniel came to the door he said, 'They're here. Let's go up and look.'

They walked up to the park. Before they even got there they heard the roar of a big diesel engine, and when they came around the corner they saw that a wide gap had been torn in the low wall surrounding the park. A huge yellow bulldozer with caterpillar tracks was forcing its way through, pushing stones and rubble before it with its great blade. It headed straight across the grass. Along one of the streets that surrounded the park a line of lorries stood waiting, each one carrying a large container like a railway carriage with no wheels.

As they stood there, a heavy truck came rumbling up the road. It had lots of big wheels with deep treads and a crane was folded on to its flatbed.

'Boom truck,' said Mike. He was a great explorer and had climbed over lots of fences; he knew most of what there was to know about heavy-duty construction machinery. 'They'll be rigging up the site offices first.'

Daniel and Mike sat on the wall of the park and watched. The bulldozer crawled backwards and forwards, flattening out a large area at edge of the park. A laurel bush and a young sycamore were swept aside and dumped like litter. Then some big dumper trucks drove straight through the gap in the wall. They turned round, churning up what was left of the grass and flower beds into a quagmire, backed into the space that the bulldozer had made and started tipping huge piles of gravel and hard core.

Next to come was a front-loader.

'Hitachi,' said Mike. 'He can take a few tons in that bucket.'

The bulldozer was hard at work, spreading hard core and then gravel over a space as big as two tennis courts. Finally, with the front-loader as assistant, the bulldozer evened out the track that it had come in on, and the two machines ground to a halt. Their drivers jumped down from their cabs and stood chatting with each other.

Now it was the boom truck's turn. It entered the park followed by the lorries that had stood patiently waiting. There was a hiss of air brakes, and then the engine revved as the crane's hydraulics unfolded the arm on its back. It lifted the portable site huts off the beds of the lorries and piled three of them on top of each other. The fourth was placed a bit to the side.

Daniel saw that they had windows and doors. On the top one was a sign saying 'Site Office', on the middle one 'Canteen' and on the lowest one 'Stores'.

On the one that stood by itself was a sign saying 'Toilets'.

Now a four-wheel-drive pick-up drove in and parked in front of the huts. It disgorged four men in yellow hard hats who started unloading scaffolding from the back. In no time at all they had bolted together the huts, and a set of steps rose up the side, with gratings to stand on in front of the doors of the top two huts.

'Pretty nifty work,' said Mike admiringly.

Just then Daniel heard a shout.

'Daniel, Daniel, are there diggers?'

Charlotte's youngest brother, Alexander, was dragging his sister towards them, while she complained, 'Take it easy, Alex, they'll be there for months.'

'But I want to see them now.'

Alexander had Heavy-Machinery Disease. An excavator making a hole in the road could put him into a trance. He could stand the whole day with his thumb in his mouth just watching. It is a disease which sometimes infects small boys and there is no quick cure. Sometimes they grow out of it. Sometimes they don't.

'Hi,' said Charlotte breathlessly. 'I didn't want to see this, but I didn't have much choice.' She looked out over the park. 'Oh no, what an ugly mess.'

'What time is it, Charlotte?' asked Mike.

'About half twelve, I suppose.'

'I've got to go. See you.' Mike sauntered off.

Charlotte lifted Alexander up on to the wall, which was taller than he was, keeping a good grasp on the back of his coat. He settled down happily and stuck his thumb in his mouth.

'They'd better come soon,' said Daniel quietly.

'They said the day after tomorrow.'

'Do you think they'll be all right in number twelve?'

'I don't see why they shouldn't be. Empty houses are just the sort of places you find ghosts.'

When they got back from Mountwood, Charlotte and Daniel had had a little conference, and Charlotte had the brilliant idea of putting up the ghosts in the Bennetts' house. Gillian and her parents had already moved out. Mr Bennett had found a job in the south; he had been wanting to move anyway, so it had seemed best to get out as soon as possible.

Alexander took his thumb out of his mouth and piped excitedly, 'The big crane, look!'

The boom truck had one more job to do that day. He had instructions from his foreman, who said they came right from the top.

He climbed into his cab, started up and drove straight across the park, ignoring paths and waste bins and flower beds and shrubbery. He stopped at the open space in the middle of the park, next to the statue of General Markham. He climbed out of his cab, unloaded a big strap and looped it round the waist of the general, who stood proudly gazing out over the city. The driver slung the other end over the hook of the crane and got back into his cab. The great boom lifted, the strap tightened, and with a wrenching sound General Sir Markham was ripped from his pedestal. He swung in the air, shedding debris and revolving slowly.

The crane drove carefully to the edge of the park, where a skip stood by the kerb on the other side of the wall. The crane's long boom lowered, and General Markham disappeared head first into the skip. Only his shattered feet stuck up over the edge.

Daniel and Charlotte watched in silence. There was nothing to say. Now everything depended on their desperate plan.

'Good,' said Jack Bluffit.

It was he who had given the order that the very first thing to be done in Markham Park was getting rid of that statue. He hated it. He was not superstitious, but he could not stand that old general standing there as though he was guarding the place. So the sooner it went, the better. There would be a much better statue standing there by the end of the year anyway.

Snyder had shown him some sketches that the sculptor had done, and he thought they were pretty impressive. No horse though. After that trip out to Ridget's place he never wanted to have anything to do with horses again, not even as a statue. They should all be turned into hamburgers, in his opinion.

'Good,' he repeated.

He was talking to the person sitting on the other side of his desk. He was called Big Robby, and the name certainly suited him. The chair he was sitting on only had room for one of his buttocks, and looked as though it would collapse at any moment. His shaved head sat like a rock on massive shoulders. There was no neck in between. Once he had been as solid as granite, but now most of him wobbled like jelly when he moved.

His real name was Robert Mayhew, and he was a multi-millionaire and sole owner of a huge construction company that had built skyscrapers and airport terminals and motorways all over the north of England. Big Robby Mayhew had started working as a hoddy on building sites in his teens, running bricks up and down ladders; he had been tougher and worked harder than anyone else, and soon he went into business for himself. It was much easier to make money that way. You could fiddle your taxes, use cheap materials and charge for expensive ones, pay low wages and scare people who complained. He knew every trick in the book, and in no time he had made his first million – the first of many.

'Yup,' he said, 'statue's in a skip. When my boys get to work they don't hang about. We'll start digging out for foundations tomorrow, and before you can say knife we'll be pouring concrete.'

'You're going to have to get a move on. That's the deal.'

Big Robby had wanted the Markham Park development job, and he had got it. But the really big payout would come if he got the job done fast. Jack Bluffit was in a hurry, with rat-face Norton sniffing at his heels and some stupid nosey parker on the council saying he had tried to pervert the course of justice by telling the police to give that old lady a going-over.

'I tell you, we work fast. We'll keep our end of the bargain,' grunted Big Robby.

The two men eyed each other across the desk. They didn't like each other. Each one thought the other was stupid. But they went way back. They had been playing around with the council's money for years, building shoddy houses and unsafe roads, and putting money in their own pockets.

The following day the excavators moved in. Alexander was in ecstasy, and Charlotte had to bring a book with her to the park. The diggers stretched and swung their great jointed necks, taking a scoop of stones and earth the size of a small car with every bite. Charlotte had been trying for about an hour to read and hold on to Alexander at the same time when suddenly he squirmed and screeched, 'It's falling over!'

One of the excavators was indeed teetering on the edge of the hole it had been digging, its caterpillars scrabbling in reverse. The driver was fast and skilful. He swung the whole body of the digger round and dropped the arm quickly, so that the toothed edge of the bucket dug into the ground. Then the powerful arm began to flex, and the digger hauled itself back from the edge. The driver hopped out of his cab as other workmen gathered round and peered down into the hole. There was a lot of shaking of heads, then one of them walked over to the site office, ran up the steps and disappeared through the door.

Big Robby was in his office when the phone rang. It was his foreman, ringing from Markham Park.

'It's like we thought, Robby,' said the foreman. 'Straight through to an old mine shaft on the first day. The whole area is riddled with old workings; they go back hundreds of years, some of them. We shouldn't be building here at all. I've said that from the start.'

'You let me worry about that. Fill it in somehow.'

'Well, I don't know. Anyway, it's going to take a long time.'

'We have a deadline to meet. And we're going to meet it. Rig up some arc lamps; we'll have to work night shifts.'

'That's going to cost you.'

'Never mind, just square it with the men.'

It would eat into his payout, but it was the only thing to do. Big Robby put down the phone and said a rude word.

Twenty-six
Team Spectre

As soon as Daniel and Charlotte had left, the Great Hagges got down to business. Organizing a posse of ghosts was just the kind of thing they were good at.

First they announced that since so many of the ghosts had applied for the mission, they would themselves make the selection, based on individual merit and value to the team. Some were bound to be disappointed, they said, but there would be other opportunities to excel.

Then they had a staff meeting. It was a proper planning meeting, and they expected it to go on for quite a long time, so Drusilla had prepared a light lunch in the Mexican style. There was a plate of crispy blowfly fritters, with a lamb-phlegm dip sauce, and toadstool sauté. When they had eaten they pushed their plates aside and got to work. Some lively discussion followed.

There were one or two obvious choices: the Peabodys for example.

'Mrs Peabody is highly gifted, and she has drive. Her interest in this situation is hardly in question. She will give of her best,' said Fredegonda.

The others agreed. It was clear that the family was a unit, and that Mr Peabody could also be relied on to pull out all the stops.

'I would suggest Kylie,' said Goneril. 'She is flighty, I admit. But we are talking of a building site, and we

201

must assume that most of the employees will be men. And men are rather her speciality.'

'True,' agreed Drusilla. 'A temptress is indispensable, I would say.'

'And also the Phantom Welder,' Goneril went on. 'I know, I know,' she said, when the other two looked doubtful, 'He has not been the most exceptional of students, but if anyone knows his way around a construction site, it is he. If he is on familiar ground it might inspire him. And he has one indubitable strength, and that is in the telekinesis department.'

The other two nodded at this. Not all ghosts can affect the material world, moving objects around or making them levitate. Some of them can do this, many can't. The Phantom Welder was no poltergeist, but he had had a good pair of hands when he was alive and had kept a strong contact with things physical even after passing over.

These were the easy choices. A long and enjoyable argument followed.

Fredegonda suggested the Legless Anglo-Saxon Warrior, on the grounds that he was crude and violent. But he had absolutely no control over his few remaining body parts, in Goneril's opinion, and what is more he was a martyr to stage fright.

Finally they settled on the Druid, who they felt deserved recognition for his sterling efforts, and the Shortener, whose materialization skills would be a valuable asset to the team.

'That seems to be it, ladies,' said Fredegonda. 'It has been a long session. I thought maybe one more team member of the grimmer variety might be useful, but I think we can be satisfied.'

The bus was booked. It would depart in the late evening, to arrive at Markham Street at midnight.

There was great excitement among the ghosts who had been chosen. They decided to call themselves Team Spectre, and although they were very modest when talking to the other ghosts, they couldn't help feeling that they were part of an elite, that they were set apart.

A final assembly had been called. The Great Hagges, sitting straight-backed and formal on their chairs, were going to address them and give them some last words of advice before seeing them off on the bus. The ghosts who had not been included were terribly disappointed, of course, but they cheered and clapped when Team Spectre glided into the dimly lit chamber, looking very serious and determined. The rest of the phantoms swirled about them, wishing them well and raising the occasional 'Hurrah!' or 'Go, team, go!' All except Cousin Vera.

She stood limply in the middle of the hall by the well-mouth. Her head hung limply, her dress hung limply, her hands hung limply at her sides. She was limp. The fat housemaster was in the middle of a pompous little speech telling Ron Peabody to 'keep a firm hand on the wheel' and 'stay the course', when Iphigenia caught sight of Vera. She excused herself, leaving Ron to say, 'Yes, of course,' and, 'Jolly good,' and glided over to her.

'Vera, Vera darling. We will be back in no time. I'm sure you will be fine.'

'I wanted to come with you,' gulped Vera, 'but there was no point in my even applying. I'm bottom

203

of the class. My wail is not. A banshee without a wail is like a . . . like a . . .' She had been about to say 'a bird that cannot fly', but then she remembered that there *are* birds that can't fly, so she burst into tears instead.

Iphigenia floated over to the Great Hagges, who were waiting for the tumult and chatter to die down before saying their final words.

'Excuse me, but could I have a word?'

'Yes, Mrs Peabody.' Fredegonda was beginning to find Mrs Peabody just a tiny bit too much. Not that she wasn't a good student, but it would be no bad thing to have her out of the castle for a while. 'What do you wish to say?'

Fredegonda's voice, as always, caught the attention of every wraith in the room. The Phantom Welder had once compared it unfavourably to the sound of a blunt hacksaw on three-quarter-inch cast-iron pipe. The crowd fell silent.

'Could not Vera accompany us? She could see to Percy while I am at work.'

'I am very sorry,' said Fredegonda, 'but this is an enterprise requiring both skill and strength of purpose. I cannot honestly say that Vera has either.'

Vera slumped in despair.

'Aa divna 'boot that. Yer niver kna.' A hoarse voice echoed from below. 'Anyways, aa'm thinkin' aa'll gan along wi'yus.'

Angus Crawe rose slowly from the depths. First his head appeared. His craggy freckled face and hollow cheeks were encircled by a straggly beard, sandy hair and side whiskers, and one could instantly see why he was a little hard to understand. Added to his rather strong accent was the fact that a Scottish claymore had at some point cloven both his upper and lower lips, so that he seemed to be wearing a permanent mad grin, showing his blackened stumps of teeth and bright red tongue.

The rest of him emerged. He was wearing only a leather jerkin on the upper part of his body, displaying a scarred chest almost as hairy as his head. The lower part of him was wearing a pair of woollen long johns. They were not very clean. He had inherited them from his father, who had never washed them either.

He floated above the dark mouth of the well and spoke directly to Vera. 'Aa'll see yer areet, petal. Nae worries.'

Drusilla spoke up. 'How nice to meet you properly at last, Mr Crawe. However, we have decided—'

Angus interrupted her. 'Divn't be daft. Aa'm gannin', and so's the lassie.' He pointed at Vera. 'Just a tick, I'll fetch up Doris.'

He swooshed back into the well, re-emerging a moment later with a huge two-handled sword that was almost as long as he was. He whirled it around his head, and it whistled and hummed. Then he emitted a blood-curdling yell, the battle cry of the Crawes.

As the echoes died away in the rafters above their heads, he said, 'Haway then. Time t'di a bit'a damage.'

At that moment the hooting of an ancient klaxon was heard from the courtyard. There was no more to be said. The Great Hagges had no time to deliver their carefully prepared speech; they bowed to the inevitable. Team Spectre, surrounded by a fluttering throng of phantoms, glided out to the bus. Last to board was Vera, accompanied by Angus Crawe.

205

Twenty-seven
The Phantom Welder

The hour approached. Just before midnight Daniel and Charlotte sat on the kerb outside Daniel's house, under a street lamp. They didn't know how the ghosts would arrive, but they had decided to be there to welcome them anyway. They were nervous and excited.

'I hope they come,' said Charlotte.

'They'll come.'

'You seem very sure.'

'I am. It's a funny thing about those Great Hagges. I mean, they are absolutely foul, and I bet they would have done something terrible to us if Percy's mother hadn't stopped them – they're capable of anything – but I can't imagine them breaking a promise.'

'Now that you mention it, neither can I.'

Just then the street lamp above their heads flickered and died. One by one all the lamps on the street went out. The temperature seemed to drop suddenly, and Charlotte shivered and pulled her jacket closer about her shoulders.

In the grubby neon glow reflected from the city sky they saw an ancient bus coast silently round the corner at the end of Markham Street. It drew to a halt in front of them. It seemed to be completely empty, apart from the driver; and even he, in his peaked cap and uniform, was whitish blue and transparent.

Slowly the bus filled with unearthly luminescence, and the various apparitions took shape and glided out of it. The first to greet them was Iphigenia, with a smiling Percy at her side.

'Well, here we are, children. How nice to see you again.'

Ronald stepped forward and stood to attention. With his pumping arteries and twitching muscle fibres he looked every bit the soldier.

'Team Spectre reporting for duty. All present and correct.'

'I think you've met everybody,' said Iphigenia. 'Except perhaps Mr Crawe.'

Angus came forward and winked. Both Daniel and Charlotte were impressed. He really did look as though he might frighten anyone, particularly when he smiled.

They said, 'Pleased to meet you,' and, 'How do you do.'

The bus moved off up the street.

'He'll have to turn round,' said Daniel. 'This is a cul-de-sac.'

'Don't worry about him,' said the Phantom Welder. 'He usually finds a way.'

The bus disappeared into the gloom and was gone.

'Now,' said Ron Peabody, 'I wonder if you could show us to our quarters. We need to set up camp and get ourselves organized before daylight. Is this the place?' Ron pointed at Daniel's front door. 'Or that one?'

'No, we waited outside my house because Percy has been here before and we thought it would be easiest to find us. And the Bosse-Lynches are next door.'

'The who?'

It was the Phantom Welder who spoke, and all his companions turned to him. He had spoken in a voice they had never heard him use before. His usual cheery expression had gone. He looked as though he had seen a ghost.

'The Bosse-Lynches,' said Daniel. 'We haven't mentioned you to them – they're not the kind of people . . .' Daniel broke off.

The Phantom Welder had drifted away, hardly visible at all.

'What's got into him?' said Ron. 'Perhaps, since we're all a bit tired and wound up . . .'

'Your house is further down, not far,' said Charlotte. 'It's empty, and we think you will be comfy there.'

'Right, off we go then.'

Daniel and Charlotte walked down to number twelve, with Percy gliding happily beside them and burbling about how he was teaching Samson to roll over and play dead.

'Here we are.' Number twelve looked dark and abandoned, in the way that houses do almost as soon as their owners have left.

'A very suitable edifice, to be sure,' said the Shortener. 'Let us enter. After you, miss.' He took off his hat and made a little bow to Kylie, who was close by. All the ghosts said good evening, and vanished. The front door of number twelve seemed to waver a bit, and then all was silent.

One by one the street lamps came back on.

*

If Daniel and Charlotte had thought about it, they would have realized that ghosts, just like cats or human beings for that matter, need their own space. In an enormous country house with a hundred rooms you might find two or even three ghosts, but mostly the rule is one ghost per churchyard, or well, or whatever. It was asking a lot of no fewer than nine to squeeze into one terraced house.

But Team Spectre was prepared to rough it. You can't expect to enjoy the comforts of home when you are out on a special mission. If you can't take a bit of hard lying, then you shouldn't be there in the first place. Soldiers have to share their bivouacs with people who pick their noses or have smelly feet; that's just part of the job. Sailors have to bunk in cramped cabins with mess-mates who are learning to play 'Greensleeves' on the mandolin or say 'down the hatch' every time they drink something. So the ghosts of Team Spectre were prepared to make the best of camping out in number twelve. But it can't be denied that it was rather a tight fit.

Already on that first night there were small irritations. The Peabodys decided to haunt the main bedroom, and there were no objections to that. The others spread themselves around the house as best they could. But the Shortener, who thought he might make himself comfy in the cupboard under the stairs, found that Angus Crawe was already in there, stroking Doris and humming quietly to himself.

Kylie and Vera both tried to get into the bath at the same time, and a lot of 'No, you take it ... No, you found it first' ended up with both of them rather rattled and neither of them in the bath.

As for the Druid, he was a wanderer by nature. They had solved the problem at Mountwood, which was very large, by giving him the whole loft space under the roof to wander about in, on condition that he didn't come down until called. But in Markham Street all he could do was wander up and down the stairs, chanting 'The Mabinogion' in lilting Welsh. That is bad enough if you speak Welsh, and close to torture if you can't. There are no phantom earplugs to stick into phantom ears.

One of the ghosts wasn't there at all. Not just invisible, but actually not there. The Phantom Welder had followed the rest of the team into the house, but while the others were floating around trying to get themselves settled, he simply melted into the wall and was gone.

After an hour or two, when the ghosts had got their sleeping arrangements sorted out, at least for the time being, it was time for a meeting to plan their strategy. They gathered in the empty living room, with its bare floorboards and marks on the wall where the Bennetts' pictures had hung.

'No time for anything tonight, I think,' said the Shortener.

'A bit of a recce, maybe, if anyone feels up to it,' said Ron Peabody. 'Just to get the lie of the land.'

'It will be night work for the most part, I suppose,' said Iphigenia, 'but perhaps some unseen activity during the day to soften them up. I thought that the Phantom Welder . . . Where is he, by the way?'

At that moment an ear-splitting scream was heard.

The ghosts vanished, and rushed to the window in time to see Mr Bosse-Lynch run down his front path, stark naked, screaming and soaking wet. Lights went on and windows were opened all along Markham Street.

The Phantom Welder knew perfectly well that they were not there to use their expert haunting skills on the innocent inhabitants of Markham Street. They were there to help them, not go wandering through the walls frightening people. But there was something he just had to do.

When he had heard the name of the people who lived at number five he had got a terrible shock, and bitter memories of the past came flooding back. Bosse-Lynch. Such an unusual name. There couldn't be any doubt about it. It was the Bosse-Lynch family that had done for him; ruined his life, and in the end killed him.

He had never told the others much about his past, he wasn't that sort of person, but he remembered it well enough. He had been a proud workman, one of the best welders in Crewe, and there were a lot of good men working there in the heyday of the great steam engines. But then came the Great Depression; the Bosse-Lynches, who owned the factory where he worked, shrugged their shoulders and sold up. Supply and demand, they said. The work was gone, and before you knew where you were you were walking the streets, rummaging through garbage bins, living on scraps and leftovers. Until one day, when he found an old newspaper with some cold greasy chips still wrapped in it. A feast to him. He didn't know that it was full of rat poison; how could

211

he? But Mr Bosse-Lynch had known, because he had put it there. The garbage bin was in the alley behind his posh house.

So now, although he knew he was letting the team down, the Phantom Welder drifted from house to house until he came to number five.

Although it was almost one o'clock in the morning, Mr Bosse-Lynch was in the bath. He had stayed up late to watch a film on television, but he still wasn't feeling very tired, so he had poured himself a large whisky and taken it into the bathroom with him, and locked the door. He would have time to pour it down the sink if Mrs Bosse-Lynch woke up.

He lay with his eyes closed, peacefully soaking in the tub, with his glass on a stool within easy reach. Without warning something cold splashed into his face and ran down his chin. He tasted whisky. He sat up and wiped his stinging eyes. He was sure he had locked the door. She couldn't have got in.

He saw his empty glass float through the air and hurl itself against the bathroom mirror, where it splintered into a thousand shards. Then the room was plunged into darkness. He saw an apparition standing by the bath looking down at him, wearing a boiler suit and carrying a welding torch. The apparition adjusted the torch until he had got the perfect mixture – the flame was sharp, dazzling blue-white, and lethal. The apparition bent down slightly, and the flame disappeared below the side of the bath.

Then the apparition spoke. 'I'll have this water boiling in about three minutes, I reckon, Mr Bosse-Lynch.'

That was when Mr Bosse-Lynch screamed.

The Phantom Welder got a proper telling-off when he returned to number twelve. The other ghosts were waiting for him in the living room.

'We agreed not to terrify our hosts,' said Iphigenia. 'What can you have been thinking?'

'I wasn't doing much thinking,' replied the Phantom Welder, who was feeling very guilty now that he had calmed down a bit.

He explained about his past. The others couldn't help but feel that he should be forgiven for his rash actions, even though when they had thought about it, and counted back on their fingers, they realized that the Bosse-Lynch whom he had terrified must be the son of the one who had killed him.

'Well, they're all the same breed, them capitalists,' he said. 'But I'll make it up to you. I'll get started right away, as soon as they start work in the morning.'

'But surely you're too tired for that now. You can't stay up all day,' said Kylie.

'Don't worry about me. I've worked double shifts before.'

There were no more secrets on Markham Street. After the Phantom Welder's little adventure the whole thing had to be explained to everybody.

Mrs Wilder and Daniel and Charlotte's parents already knew of the plan, but it came as quite a surprise to Mr Jaros and Karin Hughes and Peter and Jim. Jim Dawson, who was the kindest person you could ever hope to meet, was the one who found it hardest to accept.

'I simply do not believe in ghosts,' he said, when

Charlotte tried to explain what was going on. 'I'm a scientist, I'm not allowed to. It's against the rules.'

'Have you talked to Mr Bosse-Lynch?'

'Yes, I have. I think he has a bad conscience about something in his family's past, and he has been suppressing it; he must have had some kind of mental breakdown.'

'Would you like to meet them?'

Jim laughed. 'I certainly would, Charlotte. Bring them round any time.'

Twenty-eight
Jinxed

A large expensive car bounced up the rough track and drew up in front of the site office in Markham Park. Big Robby got out, slammed the door and took the steps up to the top hut two at a time.

'What's going on here?' he growled as soon as he got through the door.

'You tell us,' said the foreman, who was sitting at the little table covered with plans that took up most of the space. 'There's a jinx on this place.'

'Don't give me that. Incompetence is more like it.'

'How do you explain two forty-ton excavators suddenly starting to dance with each other, and their drivers just sitting there getting dizzy. It was a like a blasted funfair. How's that incompetence?'

'Those machines are so full of computer chips these days, no wonder they go haywire. Get someone on to it.'

'Done it. Couldn't find anything wrong. They're working all right now. And what about one of the caterpillars on a bulldozer stuck fast, like it was welded to the axle? It just drove round and round in circles. And then there's that.'

He got up and walked over to the window. Big Robby followed his gaze. A huge crane had been erected on the site; far out on the jib a metal plate had been fixed, with 'Mayhew Construction Ltd' painted on it. The words could now hardly be made out, because across them were scrawled the words 'Up Your Bum'.

'That's sabotage! Have those words removed.'

'Can't be done. They've been burned into the metal. Been done with a gas cutter.'

'What! How could they get up there?'

'Don't ask me.'

When Big Robby drove away from Markham Park he was furious. Jinx, eh? He wasn't buying that. Sabotage pure and simple. He would have to buy in some security; more expense, more time wasted.

The Phantom Welder was in everybody's good books now, and the others were raring to get in and play their part. They decided to start off that very night.

'We must build it up slowly,' explained Iphigenia, who had naturally enough taken on the role of artistic director. 'We must work up to a climax. Pace is everything.'

So they decided that the advance party would consist of Kylie and the Druid. The others would have a quiet night. The next night it would be the Peabodys' turn, with the Shortener. On the third night, as a grand finale, they would come in full strength.

There wasn't much to do for the ones who had been left behind. For a while they simply enjoyed the silence, now that the Druid was out of the house.

Percy quickly got bored. 'Please can I go and say hello to Daniel? Please!'

'Perceval, we have told you—'

'I'll go with him,' said Vera. 'We will be very careful.'

216

She did so want to make herself useful.

'Oh, very well.'

Vera took Percy by the hand, and they vanished. They passed invisibly through walls and across rooms until they came to number six.

'Are you sure this is the right house?' whispered Vera.

'Yes, yes, Daniel's room is at the top.'

'But I thought they were a nice family. There is something black and ugly here.'

Vera's wailing might be a disaster, but she was extremely sensitive.

Percy didn't hear her; he was already bulging out of the wall above Daniel's bed, ready to tell him all about the Phantom Welder's bit of fun, and how Kylie and the Druid were going to start the ball rolling.

Vera waited until she heard Percy's cheery voice, and Daniel's sleepy tones replying. Then she floated off. He would be all right for a while, and she really did not like the atmosphere. She glided on up the street, coming to a house which felt kind and just right for her. She could wait there for a while, and then take Percy back.

The security guard who had been hired to patrol the perimeter of the construction site took his job seriously. He led a vicious Dobermann with a spiked collar on a thick leather lead. He had lots of things hanging from his belt. A truncheon, a torch, a two-way radio. He hoped that he would catch some hooligan trying to sneak in. That would liven things up a bit. As he paced along the chain-link fence that surrounded the site his dog suddenly stopped, lowered its head and emitted a threatening growl.

'What's up, Brute? You see something?'

Then he saw it too. A hooded figure was standing in front of him, inside the fence! He instantly bent down and slipped Brute's lead.

'Get 'im, Brute!' he cried.

Brute snarled and leaped forward, his teeth bared. The figure threw back its hood, revealing a mass of golden hair and two twinkling blue eyes, which smiled at the dog hurtling towards it. Brute's snarl died in his throat. He dropped to the ground and rolled over on to his back. The mysterious figure bent down and tickled his tummy. Brute squirmed with pleasure, then fell asleep.

The security guard stood there with his mouth half open, staring at the most beautiful woman he had ever seen. She stood up and gazed at him. Then she spoke.

'We meet at last.'

'But . . . I don't know you.'

'Nor I you, and yet I have dreamed of this meeting.'

She started to walk backwards, holding his gaze all the time with her enchanting blue eyes.

The guard held out his hand. 'Stop, don't go yet,' he cried.

'Where I go, you must follow . . .'

She moved further away, still facing him, moving effortlessly over the rough ground. The guard stumbled after her. They came to a deserted part of the site, where some traces of the park still remained, a few tired laurels and a patch of grass.

Kylie called in a soft voice, 'Follow, follow . . .' and turned her back on him.

The guard's eyes widened in horror, and fear gripped him like a vice as he gazed at the empty shell that was Kylie.

She dissolved slowly into the bushes.

Charlotte's mother was in the kitchen. It was late but she thought she might as well set out the breakfast things, because any minute now little Mary would wake up and start crying. She had been having nightmares or something, and every single night, when Margaret Hamilton was desperate for bed, Mary would wake up and couldn't go to sleep again for ages. She had to be stroked and soothed, and tucked in again, and given a drink of water.

When she had finished, Mrs Hamilton sat at the kitchen table and waited. She wasn't going to be fooled this time. If she went to bed, she would only have to get up again. She waited a long time. Then suddenly, as mothers do, she started worrying. Something must be wrong. Why hadn't Mary started her wailing?

As quietly as she could, she crept up the stairs. Mary's door was ajar, as always. From inside the room a strange faint light shone gently, and she heard a soft voice singing a strange melody without words.

Mrs Hamilton opened the door. A pale, thin lady was stooping over Mary's cot. She should have screamed and called the police, but she knew at once. 'You're one of Charlotte's friends, aren't you?' she whispered.

'Yes, I am,' said Vera. 'Please don't be afraid. I know I shouldn't be here. Such a sweet child, but she was a little worried.'

Mary was sleeping like a lamb.

'How on earth did you manage it? I simply cannot get her to settle down.'

'We had a little chat, and then she felt better.'

'But she hasn't learned to talk.'

Vera only smiled. 'I should be getting back to Percy. Iphigenia will be worried. But perhaps I could visit again?'

'Of course, any time.'

Vera the Banshee faded slowly, and was gone.

Ed Bales had volunteered for the night shift. Extra money always came in handy, and Big Robby was paying in cash.

Under the arc lights that had been set up around the site he steered his big front-loader over to the huge pile of rubble and quarry waste that had been dumped on the site the day before. He scooped a load into his bucket, reversed and headed for the place where his mate had almost tipped his excavator into the old mine workings. They had to be filled in and properly compacted before the end of the shift. There was a lot of pressure on this job; everything had to be done in double-quick time.

'What's this then?' said Ed when he got to the place. 'Is someone working down there?'

A faint flickering light was visible, as though someone was using a headlamp down in the hole. He stopped and got out of the cab. Now he heard a weird chanting, which wavered up and down but never paused.

Ed looked over the edge. At the bottom of the hole, in a shimmer of pale light, stood an ancient man with long white hair and a long robe. His arms were outstretched, and his eyes under the bushy eyebrows were dark wells of red fire. Ed Bales started, and backed hastily away. Before his shocked gaze the ancient figure rose slowly to float above the hole, boring into him with its chilling eyes.

Ed was rooted to the spot. Now he could hear the chanting more clearly.

'Damned for dastardly deeds of dirty destruction
Malevolent marauders of Markham Park,
Cursed be they cruelly with crippling curses; curs,
Whipped be they wildly with thrice-bound thongs,
The ninth Druid, nastiest, deadly doom-dealer . . .'

Ed tore himself away, ran to his cab and jumped in. In desperation, fumbling with his levers, he started up, and lifted the bucket of his front-loader as high as it would go. He careered towards the edge of the hole and tipped the contents, several tons of rubble, right on top of the chanting apparition. With a thundering roar the whole load disappeared into the hole, and dust rose.

Nervously Ed climbed out of his cab and crept forward to the edge. There was nothing to be seen.

'Whatever it was, that fixed it,' he said.

But then, to his horror, a pale gleam gathered and, out of the heap that he had dumped in the hole, the Druid emerged unscathed. He was still chanting. But this time, instead of simply hovering, he glided up and advanced towards Ed, pointing a long bony finger and gnashing his tooth.

'Sense now the Stinking Druid's stench,
So served, he renders revolting revenge.'

Ed Bales heard no more. For at that moment his nostrils were assailed by a ghastly cloud of smell. The Druid had combined rotting corpses, boiling cabbage, some hellish sulphurous eggy fumes and a lot more besides.

Ed didn't even have the time to throw up. He simply collapsed unconscious.

'Now industrial accidents! What on earth is going on here?'

Big Robby was just about ready to tear his hair out. The security guard was in a psychiatric ward; any mention of Markham Park and he started on some babbling lunacy about hollow women. And now one of his best workers had collapsed unconscious. Big Robby was on the phone to his foreman.

'Isolation? Why is he in isolation? What do you mean, because of the smell? Has he come round? He has? Well, what happened? A ghost! Did you say ghost? Has everybody lost their marbles?'

He rang off. He would have to visit them himself and then talk to Bluffit. There was no way they were going to bring this project in on time.

When he arrived at City Hall, Bluffit was looking at some pencil sketches that were spread out on his desk.

'Snyder!' he roared, hastily gathering the sketches in a pile and stuffing them into a drawer. 'I told you . . . Oh, it's you, Robby. Good news, I hope.'

'Can't say it is, Jack. One problem after another.

222

Two of my employees say the place is haunted and they're not going back to work.'

'Haunted? What kind of stupid joke is that? They just want more money.'

'I offered it. They still refused.'

'Get it fixed, Robby.'

The tone of voice reminded Big Robby of what happened to people who stood in Jack Bluffit's way.

The morning meeting in Markham Street was very satisfying. Kylie and the Druid came in for a great deal of praise and admiration. So far it was going well. One more night of softening-up, as Iphigenia called it, and then, finally, the big push, a full-scale horror show that would empty the place and make sure that no one ever worked there again.

'We'll have to be on our toes if we are to compete with you two,' said Ron.

Kylie and the Druid positively glowed with satisfaction. Then as a watery sun rose over the city, and morning rush hour began to limber up, the ghosts dissolved to their well-earned rest.

Twenty-nine
Mr Jaros Waits

Rumours of strange goings-on in the Markham Park development scheme began to seep through the city. Workmen talk to each other when they have their tea breaks, and talk to their wives when they get home.

In Markham Street itself, of course, quite a few people knew exactly what was going on, and Mr Bosse-Lynch's odd episode caused a lot of talk even among those who didn't. Great-Aunt Joyce met Mrs Bosse-Lynch in the street when she was out taking the air. Mrs Bosse-Lynch was the only one among the neighbours whom Great-Aunt Joyce ever talked to. If she met Margaret Hamilton with a pushchair and a load of shopping bags she just sniffed and pretended not to see her. Karin Hughes and Mr Jaros were foreigners, and Great-Aunt Joyce had even been known to cross to the other side of the street when she saw them coming.

Now she said, 'Good morning, Mrs Bosse-Lynch, how is your husband?'

'Not very well, I'm afraid. He insists that he has had a visitation.'

'Really?'

'I know, frightfully silly, isn't it? Clearly pressure of work, or a digestive problem perhaps. He is not as young as he used to be.'

'No doubt you are right.'

A sharp-eyed observer might have seen a fleeting look in Great-Aunt Joyce's eyes that said something else.

Mr Jaros didn't give a fig for what Great-Aunt Joyce thought of him. He never had, and now she was as far from his mind as she could possibly be. So was everything else: violin bows, ghosts, Smetana ... Jessie was dying.

She might last an hour, she might last a week, but this was the end. She lay quietly on his jacket in the workshop. He had lit a fire in the stove and laid a blanket over her. She took great big difficult breaths now and then – they were more like sighs. When he knelt down to stroke her head, she opened her eyes and looked at him. There was no fear in them, and no pain. Only trust. Sometimes she made the tiniest little movement with the tip of her tail. Mr Jaros was not ready to weep yet. That would come. Now he just tried to make her as comfortable as possible, stroking and stroking her old head and speaking quietly to her.

'It'll be all right, Jess. We've had a good time together. It has to end.'

And she looked at him, and without uttering a sound she agreed.

Night fell on Markham Street, and in number twelve Iphigenia, Ron and the Shortener prepared to depart for their evening's work.

'Shall I come too? I can haunt too,' said Percy.

His mother looked at him kindly. 'I think not, dear. There are some nasty men out there. But you could recite your little poem for Vera.'

'Or do a few sit-ups,' said Ron.

Before they left, the ghosts drifted down to the cupboard under the stairs, where Angus Crawe was softly crooning an old Northumbrian air to Doris.

'Are you joining us, Mr Crawe?'

'Nae. Aa'm savin' mesel'.'

Ron shrugged his shoulders, and the ghosts departed.

When they were gone Percy said to Vera, 'Why aren't you out haunting?'

'I'm . . . I'm not very good at it, Percy.'

'Neither am I.'

Vera gave him her hand and they floated off through the wall. Percy needed to talk to Daniel, and Vera wanted another chat with little Mary.

Kylie left too. She had a little secret; she had found something absolutely wonderful in Markham Street. In one of the gardens was a silver birch, not a big one, but just big enough to be cosy in. It was such a joy to melt into it and feel herself become a part of its lissom beauty. And it whispered tales to her of her ancestral homeland, the land that she had fled when the ravishing of the forests, the clear-felling and industrialized logging, began. The birch too, it told her in its melodious whisper, had come as a little seedling to a foreign land. It understood.

The Druid remained at number twelve. He walked up and down the stairs, slowly and rhythmically reciting the ancient law of the Druids, the especially long one that he had had to learn for his initiation ceremony.

After a while Angus Crawe crept out of his cupboard and said, 'Aa've had enough of this jabbering,' and dematerialized.

Some of the night shift were having a tea break in the canteen. There were some Formica-topped tables, a cupboard with mugs and an electric kettle. A couple of scruffy posters adorned the walls. One of them was of a very curvy lady in a too-small swimsuit. The talk was of the events of the night before, particularly Jimmy's experience.

'I went to see him at the hospital, but I couldn't go in there. The stink was unbelievable. All the nurses had masks.'

'So what's wrong with him?'

'Nobody knows. But I heard him shouting, "I'll never go there again."'

'Sounds like he's been on the booze.'

'Not Jimmy. He's no big drinker. Always does a grand job.'

The last speaker, whose name was Gary, was sitting opposite the other poster, an old one advertising a film called *Destructor IV – War of the Planets*. There was a picture of a famous action film star with huge muscles and a headband. He was baring his teeth and looking ferocious.

Suddenly Gary, who had been slouching in his chair, sat up with a jerk. The film star had winked at him. He rubbed his eyes.

'What's up, Gary?'

Gary couldn't speak. He only pointed with a trembling hand.

The picture was beginning to move, and the skin was falling away, revealing muscles and blood and nerves. The face became a grinning fleshy skull; but the eyeballs, they were the worst. They twisted around in the head, all the muscles expanding and contracting, seeming to search out the room. Then their gaze fastened on Gary, and a skinless arm with bloody fingers reached out of the picture, followed by the rest of the ghastly apparition.

Ron stepped down from the wall. 'Evening, gentlemen. Who would like to go a few rounds with me?'

There was a headlong rush for the door. Pushing and shoving and even crying, the workmen threw themselves down the ladder, not caring if they fell or crushed each other in their panic. Once down, they started running, and one of them ran all the way back to his house, which was a good four miles away on the other side of the river.

Just after midnight Mr Jaros fell asleep. He was sitting in his chair by the stove, with Jessie on her jacket at his feet. Jessie was asleep too, breathing very shallowly. But Mr Jaros was instantly awake when he heard her make a little noise in her throat.

He sat up. The room was lit only by the reflected glow of the street lamp outside. Standing in the room was a tall, dark figure. It held a great sword. Both hands were cupped on the hilt; its point was resting on the floor. Mr Jaros did not really know whether he was awake or asleep. But he was not afraid.

'Have you come for my Jessie? Are you the angel of death?'

'Nae, aa'm Angus.'

'Angus?'

'Angus Crawe. Aa'm thinking of my auld Sal. She was the best. None better. Wept like a bairn, I did, when she left me. A man shuld ha' a dog.'

'When she went . . . how could you bear it?'

'Aa couldn't.'

'But what did you do?'

'Do? Nothin'. Aa just went on.'

Big Robby was in the site office talking to his foreman. They heard the thundering of footsteps from the canteen below, and the ring of heavy work boots on the metal stairs.

'They're keen to get back to work anyway,' said Robby.

His foreman didn't reply. He had had enough of this job. It was a shoddy piece of work from the start. He was no engineer, but he had lots of experience, and he knew that it was madness to put up huge buildings and build roads on this land, honeycombed as it was with old mine workings. He was hard-headed, but all these weird goings-on felt like a warning to get out while he could.

'I'm chucking it in, Mr Mayhew. You'll have to find another foreman.'

'Don't talk rubbish, man.'

'I mean it. I want out.'

'Well, forget it. I could make problems for you, and you know it.'

'You wouldn't do that. You promised.'

'Wouldn't I? You might get a knock on your door some day, someone asking where that old girl got to.'

'It wasn't my fault!'

'Wasn't it? Bit of a hurry you were in, to start demolishing those flats without checking properly.'

'But you told me to get on with it. Not to waste time.'

'I didn't tell you to swing a wrecking ball through a pensioner's bedroom window when she was taking her afternoon nap. She's in the foundations of that high-rise car park, I suppose. You get to work, my lad, and see this job through.'

Robby pushed back his chair, stood up and walked out.

It was strangely quiet on the site. The foreman couldn't hear the usual sounds of shouting and the roar of heavy diesel engines. He got up to go to the door, but just as he was about to open it he heard a tapping sound behind him.

He turned round to see a face peering at him through the window. Impossible! The site office was ten metres off the ground. The features were those of an elderly woman. Her hair was tangled and filthy, full of dust and plaster, and her expression one of anguish. The foreman backed against the wall, all the blood draining from his face, as the apparition came closer, seemed to pass through the window. Now he saw the rest of her. Dressed in a flowery nightdress, her feet in a pair of woolly bedsocks, the old lady floated towards him.

She put her hands to her wizened chest. 'Oh, I can't breathe,' she wheezed. 'Buried alive, smothered by dust and darkness. Oh the weight of it . . . the weight . . .'

The foreman burst into floods of tears and fell to his knees.

'I'm sorry, I'm sorry,' he wailed. 'I didn't know you were in there. Please . . .'

'I shall never grant you peace,' the spectre croaked, 'until you have done some good in this world.'

And then she was gone.

Iphigenia was rather pleased with the effect she had had. She would have to remind Kylie that research, a bit of careful listening before going into action, could make all the difference. Seize the moment. That was the key. And she went off to find her husband and see how he had got on.

When Big Robby walked towards his car he was deep in thought. This was without exception the worst bit of business he had ever got mixed up in. He got in, started the engine and headed off towards the works entrance. Right in the middle of the open gateway stood a man in a bowler hat.

'That's all I need,' he muttered. 'Some nosy official. Probably Health and Safety. What's he doing here in the middle of the night?'

The man didn't move until Robby drove right up to him and sounded his horn. Then he moved towards the car, with a polite expression on his face.

Robby glared at him and opened the window. 'What's it about?'

'That is a very interesting question,' replied the man. 'Very philosophical, I declare.'

For some reason the radio in Robby's car came to life. Sombre organ music was playing, reminding Robby suddenly of when his grandma used to drag him to chapel on Sundays.

'Look here,' said Robby, sticking his arm out of the

window and pointing at the man. 'I'll have you know I'm the contractor.'

'And I am the Shortener,' said the man, lifting his hat and making a little bow. 'Allow me to help you contract.'

Before Robby could do anything about it, the window of his car shot up, trapping his arm. Robby swore and struggled, but he was stuck.

The man smiled gently, reached into his inside pocket and brought out a small butcher's cleaver.

'Let me see,' he said. 'About here should do it, I think.'

He raised the cleaver high in the air and brought it flashing down.

Robby fainted.

Thirty
Number Six

Big Robby was at home. He lived in a modern house in the suburbs, with everything that someone with his money has to have. He had two expensive cars in the garage: a big expensive one for himself, and a small expensive one for his expensive wife. He didn't mind that she was expensive and had three walk-in wardrobes full of clothes, and about eight different handbags that each cost at least five thousand pounds. Rich men had to have the right kind of wife, and the right kind of car. That cost money.

Now he sat drinking very expensive Italian coffee in his kitchen. He didn't like it much. He preferred a cup of tea, the ordinary kind from the supermarket, but if you have paid a lot of money for an Italian coffee machine, and you have an Italian live-in maid who knows how to work it, then you have to make the best of it.

Robby sat at the table with the newspaper in front of him.

'Horror in Markham Park,' said the headline. Journalists just love mysteries, and ghost mysteries are the best of all. The article started, 'Is this General Markham's revenge?' and went on to quote some of his workmen.

His foreman had quit. Apparently he was going to start a charity for old ladies who couldn't afford to heat their homes properly or eat decent food. Robby wasn't going to go to the police with that old business with the wrecking ball. He had only wanted to scare his foreman into staying on. The last thing he wanted was the police poking around in his affairs.

Now he rubbed his arm thoughtfully. He couldn't believe it was still there. Had it been a nightmare? That man in the bowler hat had seemed perfectly solid, just an ordinary person. When he had come round, with his arm still stuck in the window but still attached, he had driven shakily home, determined to pack the whole thing in, whatever it cost him. But now, in the light of day . . . Big Robby was a cheat, a liar and a bully, but he was not a coward. He had the kind of grim bravery that never backs down from a fight. This time though . . . he wasn't so sure. It was one thing to take on a tough navvy in a pub brawl. But ghosts . . . How did you fight ghosts?

Robby looked out of the window and saw a sleek car turn into his driveway. He knew who that was. Jack Bluffit was paying a call. The doorbell rang, and he heard the maid open the front door.

'Where is he?'

'Mr Mayhew inna di kitchen.'

'Right then, out the way.'

Bluffit stormed in. He didn't waste time on good mornings. 'Don't back out on me, Robby. I can break you, you know I can. And I will.'

Big Robby clenched his fist, thinking how nice it would be to stand up and punch him on the jaw. Instead he said, 'You can't scare me, Jack. But I got a scare last night.'

Jack snorted. 'Don't tell me you're starting to

believe that stuff. Spooks and phantoms – I ask you.'

'Well, you explain it then,' said Robby, and told Jack about his meeting with the Shortener.

Jack calmed down while he was talking, nodding his head from time to time.

When Robby was finished he sat down at the table opposite him, leaned forward and said, 'Look Robby, it's clear enough. That was no ghost. That was someone trying to put the frighteners on you. Someone trying to muscle in on your patch. They want you to quit, so they can take over the job themselves. Don't you have any enemies in this business?'

He certainly did, lots of them. Robby thought of that big contractor from Liverpool, who, he knew for a fact, wanted to expand his business north. That man would stop at nothing.

'I think you're right, Jack. I'm not giving up yet.'

Robby felt better. Having real enemies to fight suited him fine. He had been fighting all his life.

The night was clear, and a big yellow moon rose over the city, shrinking and turning pale as it climbed into the sky, as though it was getting sadder the more it saw.

Daniel had gone to bed, but he knew there was not much point in trying to sleep. For the last two nights Percy had shown up, full of his own problems. Percy felt small and useless. In some ways this was absolutely true, and Daniel felt that Percy's parents were not helping matters at all. He was being torn in half; poetry here, gymnastics there. He had to find his own way. But Percy also told him about the ghosts' escapades in Markham Park. And tonight was the big push. It really looked as though they might succeed, if the newspapers were anything to go by.

His father had been really impressed when he read the paper that morning. 'This is incredible, Daniel. Your friends are doing an amazing job. Just make sure, will you, if I ever doubt you again, that you remind me about this.'

Daniel had felt so pleased that he didn't say anything at all.

The room went cold, and the wall beside his bed began to bulge outwards and go wavery. Daniel sat up, ready to discuss the events of the night with Percy.

'Hello, Percy.'

As soon as Percy appeared, Daniel knew that something more than usual was wrong. He looked so woebegone and worried that he was obviously about to cry.

'Are you unhappy about not being able to go along for the big push?' asked Daniel.

Sure enough, Percy burst into tears. 'There is no big push,' he sobbed. 'Nobody's going.'

'What?'

'They're just lying there. Mother and Father and Vera and everybody. They can't go. I don't know what's happening.'

'Are they ill or something?' Daniel didn't even know if ghosts *could* be ill.

'Help. You must help. I don't know what to do,' Percy wailed in despair.

'Percy, you must go and wake Charlotte. We'll think of something.'

Daniel was just trying to comfort Percy. He had no idea what he could do to help.

'Go along, Percy. I'll meet you at number twelve.'

Daniel hurried into some clothes and crept downstairs past Aunt Joyce's room. As he passed, he saw a dim light escaping from the crack under her door. Apparently she was still awake.

Daniel let himself out and ran down to number twelve.

Charlotte came quickly, barefoot and in dressing gown and pyjamas. 'I've got the key.'

Charlotte's mother still had a spare key to number twelve. She had watered the plants for the Bennetts when they were away. They let themselves into the empty hallway and opened the door to the living room.

The room was faintly lit with ghostly ectoplasmic radiance, but it was weak and unsteady, coming and going in dim waves. And it was an odd colour. The glow, which was usually bluish, was shot through with angry streaks of red and sickly yellowish green. Daniel and Charlotte could hardly make out the ghosts at all. They were not floating about as they usually did, but lying unmoving in odd places on the floor.

Kylie was sitting in a corner, with her head on her knees. Beside her was the Phantom Welder, his head back, his mouth open. The others were scattered about on the floor, apparently unable to move. Angus Crawe was nowhere to be seen.

Charlotte and Daniel crept into the room and went over to Iphigenia.

'Mrs Peabody,' said Charlotte, 'what's the matter? What shall we do?'

For a long time Iphigenia said nothing. She was

237

so weak that it was like looking at an image made of water. They could see the floor beneath her quite clearly. Then she spoke in a whisper so faint that they had to bend close to hear her.

'A plague . . . poison . . . I don't know. We are being sent on.'

'Sent on?'

Daniel turned fearfully to Charlotte. 'Can ghosts . . . ?' He didn't want to say it. 'Can ghosts die?'

'There is exorcism. I think that destroys them.'

Then something struck Daniel. 'Why is Percy all right?'

They both turned at the same time to speak to him. But Percy was gone.

The Great Hagges were in a hurry. The Rolls was going as fast as it could, with Goneril clutching the wheel and staring grimly before her, passing lorries on dangerous bends, shooting over crossroads without looking to left or right.

Fredegonda's thumb had started to prick when they were eating their breakfast that evening. At first she had dismissed it. Sometimes it did that when Vicar Flitch drove past on the main road to visit his parishioners. But it didn't stop. The pricking got stronger and stronger. Fredegonda went outside and held it up, turning slowly in a full circle. At one point, roughly east, in the direction of the city, her thumb swelled to twice its normal size and started throbbing visibly. There was no doubt about it. She went inside again. Drusilla was having a sneezing fit.

'What's going on?' she asked, blowing her nose for the fourth time.

'Our team are in trouble, I think,' said Fredegonda. 'There is no time to lose. Goneril . . .' But Goneril was already hurrying out to the car.

Now the Rolls sped through the night, reaching the outskirts of the city in record time and threading its way through the suburbs until it turned in at Markham Street and parked outside number twelve. The Hagges marched up the steps, pushed open the front door and entered the living room.

'Oh, thank God,' said Daniel when they entered.

He and Charlotte had been sitting helplessly watching the ghosts get fainter and weaker without being able to do anything to help.

'No need to thank Him, I assure you,' said Fredegonda. She took charge immediately. 'This is worse than I feared. We are under attack. This is no exorcism. Drusilla, what can you do?'

'Not much I'm afraid, unless we find the source.'

'I won't be much help,' said Fredegonda, looking at her thumb. 'There will be protection.'

'Then I fear we will lose them.'

'Lose them?' Daniel spoke up.

'Yes, lose them,' said Goneril. 'They are being sent on, disintegrated, dissolved.'

'But ghosts are already dead, aren't they? What will happen to them?'

'It is beyond our ken. But they will be ghosts no more.'

'Think, boy, think,' said Fredegonda. 'Who or what could be doing this?'

'Um . . . Jack Bluffit . . .'

'Oh, don't talk nonsense. That oaf couldn't spellbind his way out of a paper bag.'

Then they heard a weak voice, almost inaudible, from the floor by the window. It was Vera. She was in a terrible state, hardly there at all. Already most of her was just a dirty-yellow swirling mist.

They all came closer.

'What did you say, Vera?' said Drusilla. 'Try to speak.'

'Number six,' came a tremulous whisper in reply. 'Something black and ugly ... I ... I ...' But she could say no more.

'Number six? But that's where I live,' said Daniel.

'Right,' said Fredegonda. 'Number six it is. Drusilla, you stay here. Do what you can. Goneril, come along.'

In two strides she was out of the door, with Goneril after her. Daniel and Charlotte were forgotten.

Daniel ran out after them into the street. Already they were almost at his front gate.

'Wait, my mum and dad, I have to ...'

Goneril strode up to the front door, which Daniel had locked behind him when he went out. 'I've got the key,' he called, fumbling in his pocket.

But it was too late for any of that. Goneril put her hand against the locked door, and gave a little push. The lock splintered and the door swung wide.

'Hey, you can't ...' shouted Daniel, but again he was ignored.

'Upstairs, wouldn't you say?' said Goneril.

'Definitely. No more noise now.'

The Great Hagges took the steps three at a time, with Daniel stumbling after. They moved completely silently, in spite of their huge feet. On the landing they stopped.

Fredegonda pointed left, then right, at the two doors, and raised her eyebrow.

Goneril pointed to the right-hand door. A faint glow still showed under it.

'I'll go in. You keep an eye out,' said Goneril, and she pushed open Great-Aunt Joyce's door and disappeared inside.

Daniel's parents had woken up when the front-door lock splintered. Mr Salter lay awake for a moment, and then he heard a voice on the landing. He got up and stuck his head round the door. He got a shock.

Standing in front of Aunt Joyce's door, with her arms folded and a frightful expression on her face, was the biggest, gauntest, ugliest woman he had ever seen in his life. Daniel was standing beside her, looking desperate. John Salter was speechless, but Fredegonda wasn't.

'Get back inside and lock your door. And take your son with you,' she hissed.

She reached out a bony hand, lifted Daniel up by his collar, took a step forward and threw him past his father into the room. Then she gave Mr Salter himself a shove that flung him backwards to land in a heap on top of Daniel, and slammed the door shut.

Goneril looked at Great-Aunt Joyce. She was in her curlers, wearing her dressing gown and a pair of tartan slippers. She was seated on the carpet, with her legs straight out in front of her. Around her in a circle were eight small lamps, like night lights. Their smoky flames flickered in the gloom.

'I didn't expect to find *you* here,' said Goneril.

'Didn't you now?' said Great-Aunt Joyce. But her eyes were no longer the eyes of Daniel's great-aunt.

'Well, as you know, I had a spot of bother and I needed to keep out of the way, I did. And the old lady happened along just at the right time. A walking holiday in our lovely Irish countryside. So I just borrowed her, if you take my meaning, and bought myself a ticket to Stranraer.'

'And where is the real Great-Aunt Joyce?'

'In Mayo somewhere, she should be. I took her memories, of course – couldn't manage without them. She's Maeve O'Donnell now, married to a farmer.'

'Why this then?' Goneril pointed at the ring of flickering lights.

'Well, that banshee got a smell of me, I didn't like that. Anyway, I fancied a move to a place with a decent bathroom.'

As she spoke her face was changing, and she was getting smaller. Soon in front of Goneril sat a small wizened man with a trilby hat on his head.

But before she could do anything, there was no little man on the bedroom carpet. Instead a wicked-looking snake writhed there. It was a spitting cobra. Its tongue darted in and out. Then it lifted its beautiful, lethal head and spat its venom straight into Goneril's left eye. She staggered back, her eye useless.

And the snake was a snake no more. A great shadow seemed to grow in the room; a huge bear, its mouth open showing its vicious teeth, reared up and its enormous arms embraced Goneril in a frightful hug. Long sharp claws tore at her back.

Goneril was not called the Wardrobe for nothing, but she had met her match. She struggled helplessly to free her arms, to find some way of stopping the life being squeezed out of her. The bear opened its jaws wider, preparing to close them over her head.

As it did so, a hoarse shout rang out and Angus materialized in the room, the battle cry of the Crawes on his lips, his sword whizzing round his head. Doris passed through the head and body of the bear again and again. It didn't do any actual harm – it was a ghost sword – but it drove the great bear to distraction. It was worse than having a cloud of angry bees round its head, stinging and humming.

The bear couldn't help releasing one huge paw to flap and beat at the relentless blade. It was enough. Goneril freed one arm, took a large cambric handkerchief from the pocket of her skirt and wiped her eye. It flashed bright green. Instantly the bear vanished. But Goneril wasn't fooled. Peering carefully about her, she saw an earwig skittering along the skirting-board. Her green gaze found it, and fixed on it for a long time. There was a look of fierce concentration on her face. Then she relaxed.

'That should be pretty permanent,' she said.

Then she looked around, found a little pillbox on the dressing table, emptied out the pills, bent down and popped the earwig inside.

Only then could she take the time to look to Angus Crawe. There wasn't much to see. How he had managed, in his weakened and enfeebled state, to drag himself out of the cupboard under the stairs and raise his battle cry for the last time, it was impossible to say. But somehow he had done it. The blood of Starkad the Old ran in his Northumbrian veins, and no Norseman wants to die mewling in the hearth-straw. For now it was over. Goneril could see that he had given all he had. As the last wavering shadows of Angus hovered in the room, Goneril went to the door.

'Fredegonda, dear, come in. It is time to bid farewell to Mr Crawe.'

Together the two Great Hagges stood solemnly before the wispy fragments of Angus. Only his face could be made out now.

'Goodbye, Mr Crawe, we owe you our thanks,' said Fredegonda.

They heard, oh so faintly but quite distinctly and well-articulated, 'Nae bother. Ta-ra then lassies.'

And he was gone. Goneril blew her nose.

In the workshop at number four Markham Street, Mr Jaros sat and wept. Jessie was dead. She had heaved one last, tremendous sigh, wagged the tip of her tail in a final greeting to her beloved master, and the light had faded from her eyes. As he sat there in the half-light, with his heart breaking, Mr Jaros thought he heard a voice.

He raised his tearful face. It had come from outside, somewhere above the moonlit street.

'Haway then, Jess. Aa could use a bit of company.'

Then, as clear as a bell, he heard the joyful barking of a dog.

Back in number twelve, Drusilla noticed instantly that the ghosts' decline had been arrested. The shimmer around them lost its sickly hue and began to recover its normal bluish look. The Druid even sat up and started mumbling a few stanzas.

'Well done, Goneril,' said Drusilla, to nobody in particular.

Fredegonda and Goneril returned shortly after.

'That's sorted,' said Fredegonda. 'It was that tiresome Irishman, the Gruagach.'

'Wasn't he being hunted by the whole of Tír na nÓg for messing with a member of their royal family? A bit of a scandal, as I recall.'

'That's the fellow. But Goneril's fixed him. Now it's back to Mountwood, I suppose, for a bit of rest and recreation.'

'Yes, they won't be much use for a good while,' said Drusilla, looking at the ghosts, who were clearly better, but still very weak and wobbly.

Charlotte was sitting unnoticed in the corner of the room. Her heart sank.

Jack Bluffit left his house and climbed into his car. It was midnight, but he wasn't going to bed just yet.

He had sat thinking all evening. Was that Robby trying to pull a fast one? All this talk of ghosts and threats and jinxes, all the extra money that was being poured into the development. There was a scam going on somewhere; he could smell it. Was Big Robby trying to rip him off? It would be just like him. He had to have a look at what was going on, see if he could figure it out. Then he would shove it in Robby's face, and make him pay.

He left his car a few streets away and walked up to the site. The arc lamps were blazing, and men were hard at work. Robby had made a lot of calls, twisted a lot of arms, and scraped together a new crew. Tough guys they were. Jack walked round the site until he found a place where he could scramble over the fence unseen. He dropped down on the other side, and keeping low he ran to a clump of rhododendrons that still stood forlornly, surrounded by piles of reinforcing iron and discarded pallets.

Thirty-one
After the Battle

Percy stood alone, invisible, despairing, on the plinth where General Markham had been until recently. His parents were disintegrating, and waves of panic-stricken sorrow washed over him. He would be an orphan.

The work went on around him, men in hard hats shouting to each other, cranes swinging heavy girders, the thump of heavy pile-drivers slamming into the night sky. But Percy hardly noticed it. He would never be an artistic Percy now, or a gymnastic Percy, he would just be Percy. Perceval the Pitiful, the Lonely Ghost. Not his mother's Percy, not his father's Percy.

'I'll just be me,' whispered Percy to himself. 'And what use am I?'

In a sudden fury at the injustice of his fate, Percy stamped his foot.

All hell broke loose.

First came the darkness. Every light in the city went out; the blackness was thick and impenetrable. Then a vast rolling rumble filled the whole sky, followed by a furious crack of thunder. Daggers of lightning split the night, stabbing the earth beneath again and again. And now the ground in front of General Markham's plinth heaved and gaped open, exposing the angry red glare of fire. There was a roar of flames. They licked up into the darkness, and there was a foul smell of sulphur in the air.

And out of the pit they came. First, jabbering and screeching, came a horde of black-winged furies, fell creatures of the night, flapping and circling, their cruel faces and murderous eyes searching for victims, their talons spread, ready to rip and tear.

After them, creeping, crawling, leaping, came every kind of beast that ever fed man's deepest fears, and death was in their eyes. The dread Dullahan, on his black stallion, rode the air. The Fenris wolf that one day will swallow Odin Allfather at the twilight of the gods leaped from the fiery depths, threw back its fearsome head and howled.

There was a hissing of serpents, and Medusa the Gorgon, with writhing snakes for hair, rose from flames. She stared with her baleful eyes – the look that no man may meet, for it turns him instantly to stone.

Jack Bluffit was still in the rhododendron bush. He had been thrown on his back when the thunder roared and the ground shook. He lay there, terrified, as unearthly screechings and the roar of flames filled the air. He had to get away. He rolled over on to his stomach and started crawling. He stood up, prepared to step out of the bush and make a dash for safety. He peered through the foliage. He saw total desolation, illuminated by the red glare of the fiery pit. The entire site was a shattered, smouldering wasteland.

Jack was filled with a mad, unstoppable rage. He clenched his fist and shook it in fury at the destruction of all his plans and schemes. He heard a hissing sound, and looked straight into a pair of unfeeling, staring eyes.

The bus was on time. On the stroke of midnight it turned into Markham Street and drew to a halt outside number twelve. The ghosts, fully restored, were gliding about saying their farewells. There was not much excitement and laughter, only the quiet partings that mark the aftermath of battle.

The loss of Angus Crawe had been hard, even though they knew he had chosen the hero's way.

Everybody was there, even the Bosse-Lynches. The Phantom Welder floated over to them. Mr Bosse-Lynch flinched slightly, but he stood his ground.

'Shall we let bygones be bygones?' said the Phantom Welder.

'Yes,' said Mr Bosse-Lynch. 'I understand you had a rough deal. And you have saved our homes.'

'Credit goes to young Percy, I'd say.'

All the ghosts had been stunned when they found out that in their midst was a hell stamper. They had only heard rumours that such spectres existed. As far as any of them knew, the last one known to walk the earth had been over two thousand years ago, when a whole Greek island had disappeared beneath the Aegean Sea. Ron Peabody was so swollen with pride that they thought he might explode, and Iphigenia was not much better. And neither of them, really, could put Percy's success down to poetry or physical exercise. He was what he was.

The hell-stamper himself was saying tearful goodbyes to Daniel and Charlotte. 'You will come to see us? Please say you will. Samson wants to see you too. The Great Hagges won't mind, I'm sure.'

Daniel and Charlotte weren't as sure as Percy, although when the Hagges had left earlier, Fredegonda had said, 'For children, you are not too bad. I've seen worse.'

Then Daniel had got the courage up to ask, 'Er . . . Great-Aunt Joyce . . . ?'

Fredegonda had just looked at him.

Then she climbed into the Rolls and said, 'Goneril, that reminds me. Stop at the post office on the way home, will you? We have a little parcel to send to Ireland.'

As the Rolls, that nóble triumph of British engineering, accelerated smoothly away, Goneril declared, 'My goodness, I'm starving after all that exercise. I could eat a horse.'

Drusilla leaned forward and poked her nose over Goneril's shoulder.

'It's funny you should say that . . .'

Now it really was time to go. As Kylie got on to the bus she gave Karin Hughes a shy little wave and whispered, 'Thank you. Thank you for the tree.'

Margaret Hamilton hurried up breathlessly, with Mary on her arm. 'Oh, thank goodness you haven't left. She just won't settle down. I think she wants to say goodbye to Vera.'

At that moment they all realized that Vera was not with them. She had been the slowest to recover, and was still nothing like her former self. The loss of Angus had almost broken her fragile spirit. And now she had disappeared.

Then, from high above the rooftops of Markham

Street, an unearthly sound was heard. It started as a sort of sighing moan, and then got louder and louder, becoming an eerie, heart-stopping cry that rose and fell and rose again; it bore all the sorrows of the world and cast them to the sky. Then it fell silent.

After a moment Vera materialized, wiping her nose.

'I have wailed,' she said. 'For Angus.'

Then she turned to where Margaret Hamilton was standing with her baby on her arm. 'Goodbye, little Mary,' she said, and leaning over she whispered something into her ear. Mary gurgled happily.

The bus finally departed. Peter Richards and Jim Dawson watched it go.

'What on earth am I going to do now?' said Jim. 'I don't believe in ghosts.'

'Freak Storm Puts an End to Markham Park Development', read the headline.

In smaller letters underneath it said, 'Council to finance affordable homes on country estate.'

Daniel and Charlotte were sitting on Mrs Wilder's sofa, taking it in turns to read aloud to her while she poured out the tea.

Inside the newspaper they read, 'Star journalist Sam Norton exposes corruption in City Hall.'

There was a very long article all about how huge expensive projects had led to wanton destruction of the city – and all to line the pockets of entrepreneurs and civil servants. The article ended, 'But where is the spider in this web of deceit and lies? Where is Jack Bluffit?'

'Where indeed?' said Mrs Wilder. 'Probably in Rio

251

de Janeiro enjoying his ill-gotten gains.'

Charlotte glanced at Daniel, and then she said, 'Mrs Wilder, what about a walk up to the park? Just to see what's happening.'

'Well, if you think you can get me there, that would be very nice.'

So the three of them walked slowly to Markham Park, Charlotte on one side of Mrs Wilder and Daniel on the other, just in case.

Already the restoration had begun. There were lots of volunteers from the streets around the park, digging flower beds and putting in new plants. The leader of the council had decided that General Sir Markham's wishes should be respected. 'In perpetuity means just that,' he had declared. There was an election coming up.

Daniel and Charlotte led Mrs Wilder to the edge of the park, where a rhododendron bush that had somehow weathered the disaster stood by itself. Partly hidden by the new foliage stood a statue. It was of a man shaking his fist in fury at General Markham, who had been rescued from his skip and now gazed proudly over the city from his plinth.

Mrs Wilder studied it in silence for a while.

'Well, children,' she said eventually, 'they do say that you should be careful what you wish for. One day your wish might come true.'

They turned for home. They came to the iron posts and walked on down Markham Street. As they approached Mr Jaros's house they heard voices raised in furious argument.

Mr Jaros and Peter Richards were sitting on the

front step. At their feet, lying on Mr Jaros's jacket lay Angus, the puppy who had arrived only a few days earlier. He lay fast asleep with his paws in the air and his tummy warming in the sunshine. He was oblivious to the battle raging above him.

'He has the speed, and he has the technique, I tell you. He is really top class.' Peter sounded very worked up.

'Nonsense!' cried Mr Jaros, dragging the fingers of one hand through his hair and waving the other one about. 'I say pooh to that. He is flashy, he is young and pretty, but it takes more than that to make someone great.'

'I bet you, in five years they will be calling him a genius.'

'Never, not in fifty years.'

The children walked past with Mrs Wilder. It seemed better not to disturb the argument.

'Dear me,' said Mrs Wilder. 'I suppose it's about that violinist who played at City Hall last night.'

'No, it's not,' said Daniel, who had been round at Mr Jaros's finishing off Charlotte's box earlier that morning. 'They're arguing about the Argentinian midfielder that United has just bought. They've been at it for days. When they get tired of it they'll start arguing about music again.'

Mrs Wilder sighed contentedly. It was as it should be. You can only have a furious fight about nothing at all if you know that your home will still be there tomorrow.

About the Author

Toby Ibbotson is the eldest son of award-winning author Eva Ibbotson, whose novel *The Abominables* he edited with her first publisher, Marion Lloyd, following his mother's death. *Mountwood School for Ghosts* is his debut novel, from an original idea by Eva and planned out in detail by the two of them before her death. Containing all the warmth, humour and spark of Eva's novels for younger readers, which are being rereleased alongside this publication, *Mountwood School for Ghosts* marks Toby out as an exciting new storytelling talent in the children's book world. He lives in Sweden with his family and writes whenever he can.

'What joy to find the rare spirit of Eva Ibbotson lives on, perfectly rendered, through her son Toby. *Mountwood School for Ghosts* shimmers with the wit, style and special sense of fun of the very best kind of children's book'

Amanda Craig

About Eva Ibbotson

Eva Ibbotson was born in Vienna, but when the Nazis came to power her family fled to England and she was sent to boarding school. She became a writer while bringing up her four children, and her bestselling novels have been published around the world. Her books have also won and been shortlisted for many prizes. *Journey to the River Sea* won the Nestlé Gold Award and was runner-up for the Whitbread Children's Book of the Year and the Guardian Children's Fiction Prize. *The Star of Kazan* won the Nestlé Silver Award and was shortlisted for the Carnegie Medal. *The Secret of Platform 13* was shortlisted for the Smarties Prize, and *Which Witch?* was runner-up for the Carnegie Medal. *The Ogre of Oglefort* was shortlisted for the Guardian Children's Fiction Prize and the Roald Dahl Funny Prize. Eva Ibbotson died peacefully in October 2010 at the age of eighty-five.

THE BEASTS OF CLAWSTONE CASTLE

EVA IBBOTSON

'They ought to be in the country,' said Mrs Hamilton.
'It's where children ought to be.'

When Madlyn Hamilton and her younger brother
Rollo are sent by their mother to stay with their
Uncle George at crumbling Clawstone Castle, they
can see that action is needed before the castle falls
down completely! With the help of a team of
scary ghosts – including Mr Smith, a one-eyed
skeleton, and Brenda the Bloodstained Bride – they
hatch a spooky plan to save their new home. But
with a sinister scientist after the estate's prize
cattle, money might not be enough to save the
mysterious white beasts of Clawstone Castle . . .

MONSTER MISSION

EVA IBBOTSON

'We must kidnap some children,' announced Aunt Etta.
'Young, strong ones. It will be dangerous,
but it must be done.'

Three children – Minette, Fabio and Lambert –
are stolen and taken away to a bizarre island, home
to mermaids, the strange and enormous boobrie
bird, selkies and the legendary kraken.
But soon the children find themselves in great
danger as the island is under siege from a wicked
man with plans to use these extraordinary
creatures to make money. Can the children
save themselves and their new friends?

THE SECRET OF PLATFORM 13

EVA IBBOTSON

*'Well, this is it!' said Ernie Hobbs, floating past
the boarded-up Left Luggage Office and coming to rest
on an old mailbag. 'This is the day!'*

Platform 13 at King's Cross Station hides a
remarkable secret. Every nine years a doorway
opens to an amazing, fantastical island and its
occupants come visiting. But the last time the
doorway was open the island's baby prince was
stolen from the streets of London. Now, nine
years later, a rescue party, led by a wizard and an
ogre, is back to find him and bring him home.
But the gentle prince seems to have become
a spoilt rich boy, and he doesn't believe in
magic and *doesn't* want to go home.
Can they rescue him before the doorway
disappears forever?

WHICH WITCH?

EVA IBBOTSON

*'And remember,' he said, throwing out his arms,
'that what I am looking for is power,
wickedness and evil. Darkness is All!'*

Arriman the Awful, feared Wizard of the North, is
searching for a monstrous witch with the darkest
powers and is holding a sorcery competition to
discover which witch is the most fiendish.
Glamorous Madame Olympia conjures up a
thousand plague-bearing rats, while Belladonna,
the white witch, desperately wants to be a
wicked enchantress, but only manages to
produce flowers not snakes. Can she become
more devilish than all the other witches?